Dog Tales

By

Jim Dustin

To Dick and Maggie —
who forgot to bring
me a pie.
Jim Dustin

This book is a work of fiction. Places, events, and situations in this story are purely fictional. Any resemblance to actual persons, living or dead, is coincidental.

ISBN: 1-4140-1025-7 (e-book)
ISBN: 1-4140-1024-9 (Paperback)
ISBN: 1-4140-1023-0 (Dust Jacket)

Library of Congress Control Number: 2003097743

This book is printed on acid free paper.

Printed in the United States of America
Bloomington, IN

Illustrations by: Karen Miller

1stBooks - rev. 12/18/03

Dedication

I would like to dedicate this book to my mother, who never got to read it. She died of the infirmities of age just as I was finishing it.

Preface

I began writing these dog tales as a solace for my wife, who was extremely, perhaps overly attached to her dogs. All of the dogs in these stories have lived on this earth as largely as they live in my mind. Three are alive today and watching me as I write.

Two of them probably won't live beyond the year. There should be a law in the universe that requires that man and dog die at the same moment. A dog's life is so much shorter than ours that it is almost certain that we will live on after having experienced the loss of our best friend, a friend who does not care if we're white or black, Christian or Muslim or Hindu, handsome or ugly, early or late, tall or short, or even good or bad.

We should not have to have them with us for 5 or 10 or 15 years, then lose them, only to live on with the memories of what good pups they were. Nor should they have to lose us in some idiotic event like a car accident and wonder, day after day, why their human hasn't come home, wondering if they've done something wrong to be so punished.

But mostly, dogs go first. Maybe they were designed like that. Most people had their first dog when they were children. Most of them lost their first dogs when they were teens. Maybe one of the many favors dogs do for us is to teach us about death at an early age when otherwise, we would be unlikely to encounter it.

Later in life, when we experience the death of a parent, or a wife, or a child, we have already been introduced to the tragedy by a lesser, but no less noble being. We have been vaccinated, so to speak, against grief, and are perhaps better prepared to handle it.

That is reality, but I prefer to consider more than the reality of what we can touch or see or prove to exist. In my realities, dogs go to their rewards in much the same way that we humans hope to.

And who's to say I'm wrong?

Jim Dustin

Walden, Colorado

March 14, 2003

Table of Contents

DOGS : DOMESTIC
KM

Sam

Amongst the 96 trillion levels of Heaven, one level was assigned to Dogs (Domestic, house). Dogs being dogs, that level represented one of the more pleasant domiciles of the afterlife were one able to visit such levels without having performed the admission prerequisite of dying. Dogs (Domestic, house) was a friendlier place than, say, Dogs (feral), or Hyenas, or Snakes (venomous, neuro-toxic).

While we may not be able to comprehend why a black mamba might achieve a state of grace, we can readily believe that not only do all dogs go to heaven, they all go prematurely. They die before we do, and we think that's unfair. So during our hypothetical tour of the 96 trillion levels of Heaven, we would want to visit Skippy, or Spot, or Scamp, or whoever, and we would go to Dogs (Domestic, house). But we might be put off somewhat by the top dog at this level.

The overseer of this particular level was Abelard Belasarius, who had been a giant and fearsome looking mastiff during his Time on earth. Even in heaven, he appeared to be a fearsome brute, and our hypothetical visitor could readily believe that this dog was in charge. In fact, one could readily believe that this dog was in charge of Level: Wild Boars, or Level: Marauding Things of the Night.

Abelard Belasarius had been bred as a war dog and trained to fight in the tumultuous Dark Ages of earth when life was cheap and mercy rare. From such an age comes the phrase, "Shout Hurrah! And unleash the Dogs of War!" These great canines went into battle alongside their masters and viciously attacked both opposing horses and men. They were savage beasts, bred for size and ferocity. One might describe them as fearless, but dogs are not fearless. They are courageous, able to perform such feats despite their fear. But most dogs would rather not do what Abelard was trained to do, and as it happened, Abelard didn't like to do what Abelard was trained to do. So Abelard didn't do that.

Later ages would have described the big dog as a big wussy. Abelard, despite his large size, ferocious demeanor and imposing name, had no desire at all to kill humans or attack horses. Ordered to perform, he would sink to his belly, look fearfully at the oncoming foe, and look back woefully at his master, hoping for further instructions. Less intelligent masters would have given up on Abelard then and there, but his breeders recognized that Abelard's good points were in his genes, not in his behavior. And so this dog achieved a sort of heaven on earth before he achieved heaven in heaven by virtue of his assignment to pass along his genes to other dogs through similarly endowed females of the species. And when his Time passed, Abelard died. And because The Proprietor judged his life virtuous (celibacy not being a criterion), the big dog entered heaven and became overseer of Level: Dogs (Domestic, house).

This being Heaven, overseers really didn't have much to do except to do what made them happy. When Significant Movements were in the wind, the orders came from On High and were always acceptable and always carried out.

And such orders were carried out enjoyably because it is the nature of Heaven that all residents, having spun out their earthly skeins in an honorable and righteous manner, were granted their just rewards, and most simply wanted contentment. For some dogs on this level, contentment meant pulling sleds across a frozen tundra or carrying a pack in the mountains. For others, it meant lying on the porch all day with the expectation of dinner lingering in the backs of their minds. For some, it was dinner.

It didn't matter. The Proprietor had resources enough and more for all tastes and desires. And if a few duties were required along the way on this particular level, it was simply the nature of dogs to enjoy carrying out those duties.

Now, one might observe that Abelard was not exactly overloaded with the aforesaid duties. He had a great deal of time available. Time is a nebulous concept for dogs. Lying around all day, for instance, does not represent a waste of time in Dogdom. In reality, they are watching cars go by, sampling intriguing scents in the air, listening to the nearby robin fly, hearing sounds we cannot hear. They could be lying there solving all the earth's problems, but not knowing how to communicate to us that they've done that. We'll never know.

Abelard, at the moment, appeared to be en route to lying around all day. In actuality, he was utilizing the expanded senses available to one of his heavenly state. He was observing a scene in real time on the real earth. In this scene, a dog strode purposefully along the median of an interstate highway. He was scared unto death at the speeding, smelly vehicles on either side of him and so remained on the cool grass of the median.

When the median came to an end at a hard, white wall, the dog turned and retraced his steps in the opposite direction. If he kept going, he thought, he'd pick up master's scent and go home. He didn't know why master had left him out here, but he was hungry and tired and scared.

So he kept going, and kept going, and kept going though he was hot, tired and thirsty. We have observed that dogs don't possess much of a sense of time, but this particular dog felt his time was running out. He wouldn't even have minded the situation if master was here, but in addition to all the other discomforts, he was very lonely. Therefore, when one of the big smelly vehicles stopped near him, he didn't get angry or scared right away.

Facing the vehicle, he saw a human emerge and at first whiff, decided she didn't smell dangerous.

"Poor puppy. Somebody left you out here. Poor puppy. Come here puppy. It's okay, come here. Are you hungry? You're thirsty, aren't you, poor puppy."

The dog was inclined to snarl, but indecision interfered. Master wasn't around to protect. Master wasn't around to tell him what to do. The dog compromised by backing away from the slowly approaching human.

"Aw, it's okay puppy. I won't hurt you. Poor puppy. Would you like a sandwich? Are you hungry? I know what you want," and she ran back to the car.

The dog didn't run. His nature included an inherent trust of humans. He had obediently "stayed" as his master told him, stayed until he couldn't see master's car any more, stayed for, it seemed to him, beyond the confines of the command. The dog looked around, hoping master would appear to tell him what to do.

But it was the female human who returned. "Here puppy, here's something for you." The dog gazed at her with longing. She held the hard cold water in her hand, and the dog was desperate for it. He began panting heavily in the heat of expectation. He took a couple of tentative strides toward her. "That's good, puppy. It's okay. I won't hurt you."

He wished she'd drop the hard cold water and back away, but she knelt down to face him on his own level. That helped. He sidled a little closer, and her constant soothing chatter began to allay his fears.

He was close enough that he could feel the cold radiate against his nose. He was very thirsty. Remembering his manners, he gently took the hard cold water from her upturned hand. It was so good! He could feel the cold etch a trail down his throat and permeate his body. But it was gone already. He looked at the human crouched in front of him. Moisture still glistened on her palm.

The dog eased up to her and licked her hand, tasting the salt and filling his nostrils with her scent. It was a good scent, he thought. "You don't have any collar, honey. Do you want to come with me? We'll find you a home. Good dog, good puppy. Come with me, puppy," she said, exposing more hard cold water in her other hand.

The dog reached what was - for him anyway - a sort of epiphany and followed the human into the vehicle. He really did like to ride in cars. There was a male in the car, but it wasn't master, The dog whimpered a little, partly in fear and partly in the realization of abandonment. He looked up with an expression of doggy hope to the female. She responded with a smile and scratched his ear. He felt better.

He heard the humans conversing, but didn't understand. His head perked up every once in a while when he recognized a word, but mostly he just wanted to sleep.

"Well, that only took 45 minutes."

"Rickie, somebody dumped him there. He would have been killed!"

"I know, honey. I know." Rick really couldn't be mad for any appreciable length of time at the woman he loved. This episode with the stray dog was one of the reasons he loved her. This would be about the 50th dog she'd rescued from some sort of dire fate, counting the three at home. This one would go to the Humane Society. The dog was cute as a, well he was as cute as a puppy, and this puppy would yank at someone's heart, and it would find a home.

The fact that he was seriously late for a business appointment didn't bother him much. If his associates couldn't handle the reason for his tardiness, he could do without such associates. His wife Jeannie's happiness was far, far more important. He glanced at her, kneeling backwards on the passenger seat, cooing to the dog, smiling as she watched the little tyke try to keep its eyes open.

"And don't call me Rickie," he commented, more to himself than to her.

They were a pair, these two. He hadn't married until he was 42 years old, having had a series of unfortunate love affairs that took him to a point where he was misogynistic enough to call dating socially acceptable prostitution.

"What's the difference," he would tell his friends at the bar. "You spend $50, $100 for a dinner, $50 for drinks, $30 for a show, whatever for gas and maybe flowers. Most guys spend that in the hopes of getting laid at the end of the evening. You could get a decent hooker for $250 and dispense with all the nonsense and game-playing."

Rick was still looking for a partner, but not seriously, convinced that the women in America wouldn't know true love if it walked up and poked them in the eye. Maybe he'd read too many King Arthur books when he was young, or maybe he was influenced by his parents being married 59 years until only death did part them. But he had become one cynical dude.

Then there was Jeannie, married when she was 18, divorced when she was 24, married when she was 28, divorced when she was 35. During the marriages, both husbands had cheated on her. Between the marriages, she had gone out with a succession of jerks. After her last marriage, she had expected to go out with another succession of jerks until she met Mr. Right, and was getting a little worried about losing her looks before that happened.

She had happened to walk into the bar when Rick was making his comment about socially acceptable prostitution, got into a conversation with him about it, and pretty soon, they were dating. Pretty soon after that, they were married.

She was a redhead with a horrible temper that she could unleash on anyone except Rick. If she got mad at Rick, he'd just retreat to some sanctuary - his study, usually. Jeannie was mortally afraid that he would one day just retreat out of her life, and so saved her temper for work. She could only manage to keep a job for a few months at a time.

Rick didn't care. He made enough for both of them. Whatever Jeannie earned, she blew on the dogs. Rick loved having dogs, never having been able to have them as a kid because of his mom's allergies. Jeannie would not only buy them the best food and medical care, but doggy coats and doggy boots for the winter, toys every Christmas, chew bones, regular bones, whatever.

And she would volunteer with any agency that helped dogs, even though that took a toll on her. She'd come home crying from Pets-Mart after having spent the day watching person after person walk by dogs up for adoption, dogs trying desperately to catch the eye of a passerby.

"Honey, most of the people going to Pets-Mart already have dogs. It's not surprising so few stop," Rick would say.

"I know," she'd sob. "It's just so sad, watching those little guys all day. They want so much to have a home."

Abelard viewed the scenes of their lives with the big, dark eyes of his breed, stretched out on his stomach with his awesome head resting on the point where his two front paws were pressed together. Viewed from the front, he looked as if he consisted only of a head attached to two feet. He let forth a great sigh of contentment, the picture of two humans saving an abandoned member of his species having pleased him mightily.

While Abelard definitely was not overworked, he did have some responsibilities. Along with such responsibilities came certain privileges. It was given to such inhabitants of heaven certain powers beyond what they had enjoyed on earth. Abelard didn't usually exercise such powers; they scared him. He was, after all, a dog, not a nuclear scientist. But watching Rick and Jeannie's life on earth had given him such joy that he did what dogs often do, tried to gobble up more than was good for him.

The overseer dog was able to see into the future, and watching Jeannie gave him such pleasure that he began to look further and further into the future, unable to wait for the next days' events to unfold in their proper time. The dog scrolled the coming days and months through his mind like a feature film. He imagined himself in the role of one of their three dogs, the husky, the Newfoundland or the white German shepherd. ("Rickie," she had said, "People won't adopt big dogs. We've got to take them." Rick had glared at her, trying to resist those big eyes set in a pixie face. Having lost on all fronts, he insisted, "Okay, okay…but don't call me Rickie." Her worried frown morphed into a dazzling smile. "I won't, I promise. Oh, thank you honey. Thankyouthankyouthankyou!")

Abelard looked around somewhat guiltily and scrolled forward further into the future - months into the future, and then years. The big dog watched Jeannie arrive home one day in her little red car, perfect in every little detail except the smashed front end. Instead of running to the front door when she got home, Jeannie ran to the back yard and let her three dogs out. She got back to the front about the same time Rick came storming out the front door, staring in disbelief at the damaged car. She huddled among her big dogs. The dogs had no idea what was going on, but they knew it wasn't normal. They pressed in around their mistress, enveloping her in an armor of fur and looking worriedly at Rick.

Rick was mad. He'd told her a gazillion times not to tailgate; he'd told her she drove too fast; he'd told her they couldn't afford a wrecked car.

From amongst the roiling bodies of fur came a small voice: "Rickie fix?"

Rick felt his mad evaporate. After all, she wasn't hurt. "Damn it," he said, and went and dug her out from among the dogs and hugged her. The dogs ran full speed in tight circles around the pair, tongues hanging out of smiling mouths.

Abelard loved this!

He suspected what he was doing was wrong, but he kept watching further into the future. For him, time was meaningless. For Rick and Jeannie, years passed. And it was time for one of their vacations. "Backpacking, Yes!" Jeannie had decided for them both.

"Big surprise," Rick thought. It was either the sea for the Newf, the farm for the shepherd or backpacking for the husky. They couldn't afford expensive vacations, and anyway, it was hard to find a resort that would allow dogs, so they were campers by economic and social necessity. They would head for places where other humans were few and the dogs could run until happily exhausted.

He'd had a very good backpacking tent - a gift from his parents - for years. Getting ready for the trip, he'd set up the tent in the back yard to seal the seams and air it out. Sometime during the night, the shepherd and the Newf, exiled to the yard because of a lapse in their inside manners, had a major disagreement.

Newfoundlands weigh in at around 140 pounds; the shepherd mix was around 80. It was a hell of a fight, and the tent unfortunately got in the way. Jeannie and Rick looked at it the following morning. The fly was ripped, shock rods broken, holes in the floor. "Rickie fix?" Jeannie said.

"No, Rickie can't fix! We're not rich, you know," Rick exploded. "That's a $350 tent. It lasted 10 years until these stupid dogs got a hold of it. It's wrecked, it's garbage," and he stalked back into the house.

Jeannie looked at the mess and absently patted the Newf's big head. "I know you guys didn't mean it, but you've got to stay away from his stuff." She cringed at the memory of Rick coming out and finding his electric drill chewed into uselessness by one of the dogs (the guilty party never having been identified). "We've got to make this up to him," she had said about the drill.

And she had, secretly making and selling at work little cat toys made with fresh catnip that she grew in her herb garden. Eventually, she'd earned enough to buy Rick a professional electric drill that was far better than the one that was ruined. He found it in a sloppily gift-wrapped box when he came home one night.

There was a card with paw prints on it that said, "Rick, we're sorry we ate your drill. We attacked a tool guy and got this for you."

The tent was another matter. She didn't have an extra $350, and they were leaving in a week. This could put a damper on the whole vacation because Rick would have to pay a premium to order a tent and get it delivered on time. You just couldn't go out and buy an ultra-lightweight backpacker's tent at the local Wal-Mart. And he hated charging stuff. Rick was strictly a pay-as-you-go person.

He'd left for work when she ventured back in the house. She cleaned everything. She even cleaned his workshop, taking pains to put all the tools back where they were when she started (and away from the dogs.) Rick said he never could find anything after she cleaned. She mowed the lawn (which she never did) and did all the little tasks she told Rick she was going to do but never got around to doing. She made a magnificent dinner, and had a vodka tonic with a lime twist waiting when he got home.

He was stunned.

He sat down on the couch and said, "Jeannie, come here. Sit down."

"Jeannie, I'm not going to stop loving you because the dogs ate the tent. We'll manage. We've got a lot of time to spend together, and when we look back on this, it won't be a big thing. It won't be anything at all. You didn't have to do all this."

"But you were so upset!" she said.

"I'm human. And I'm sorry I'm not rich, and I'm sorry we've got old cars. I'm sorry I can't give you a better life. I wasn't angry at you. I was angry at me for not being more of a go-getter. I was angry, but I just needed some time to get over it, to put things in perspective. I'm sorry I yelled at you. I love you, you know."

"I love you too, you know," she said, hugging him close.

"I love you both," Abelard thought.

A week and a half later, Rick and Jeannie were scrambling down the face of a mountain ridge in the Mount Zirkel Wilderness Area of northern Colorado. Rick had just coaxed Jeannie into walking up an 11,500-foot peak along the Continental Divide. It was a magnificent sight, and a magnificent feeling standing atop a mountain and seeing the tops of mountain ridges marching away like waves into a clear, western sky. She felt like she'd never been this high, physically or emotionally. She felt good, and fit, and slightly exhilarated by the proximity of those cliffs and the strong wind working steadily in its never-ending task of scouring the mountaintop.

“What attracted you to me in the first place, Rick?” she asked. Jeannie looked fresh and clean and happy standing there, her flowing hair framed by a perfectly blue sky unsullied by a single cloud.

“Your legs. It was summer, and you were wearing those denim shorts, and a crisp, white shirt,” Rickie said.

“My legs. Thought so,” she said, checking on her dog.

She caught her breath at the sight of her husky running at full speed along the edge of precipitous cliffs as if there was no danger at all. The husky was a goof - a big, overly friendly, indestructible and inexhaustible goof. Jeannie, of course, loved him. “Rick, can we go down now? Buck is scaring the poop out of me.”

“Well, I think there’s a regulation against doing that in a Wilderness Area. Anyway, I’m starving. Let’s go.”

They’d taken the easy way up, a long, circuitous route along faint trails that ran by their camp. The mountain ridge hung over the valley below in a giant U shape. They’d walked the long, easy grade around the arms of the U to get to the top. Rick led them on a shorter route down. It was a jumble of boulders, many as big as houses, piled in a long avalanche track down the east side of Mount Ethel. It would have been a tough climb up, scrambling up and over the big rocks. Scrambling down was easier.

Above them, hanging off the side of Mount Ethel, was a 400-ton squarish hunk of rock that leaned away from the peak. This hunk had begun life as a part of Ethel, but the ebb and flow of seasons with the accompanying temperature differentials had developed a tiny crack between the mountain and her calf.

Every year, a little water seeped into the crack, froze, and expanded, making the crack slightly wider. Not much, but a little. A little wider, an imperceptible gain year after year, century after century, millennium after millennium until the monolith was separated from the mother peak by a distance of several feet. It looked as though it ought to fall over, but it was solid. Heedless rock climbers had actually ascended it.

But time is a tireless leveler. The vast pile of jagged boulders below the peak bore silent witness to this fact. The monolith was overbalanced, and on this particular day, Aug. 23, 2000, as Rick and Jeannie clambered down the slope below, it tipped a fraction of a degree too far and gravity's greedy hands reached up and took hold, pulling the great rock over and down toward the bosom of the waiting earth.

Its fall began so slowly that it made little sound. But when it broke away from the mountain, the groan of its separation filled the valley. Rick looked up and, recognizing the event in progress, froze in horror. The whole boulder pile shifted with the weight of the monolith striking, and he and Jeannie were thrown violently in opposite directions.

Some time later - he didn't know how long - Rick regained consciousness and automatically began a limb check. Outside of a monumental headache and uncounted contusions, he seemed to be all right.

"Oh my God," he thought. "Jeannie! Jean!"

He heard a small sound from about thirty yards away. He scrambled over the boulders toward that sound. Arriving, he found Jeannie amidst the rock slide.

Rick knelt down beside her. He could see right away that one of her beautiful legs was crushed beneath the weight of a boulder the size of a UPS truck. It looked as if her leg was one with the rock, so tight was the seam between the upper and lower boulders. "Oh, Jeannie, I am so sorry. It should be me lying there. Oh please, make this not have happened!"

Jeannie, flickering in and out of consciousness, knew things were worse than Rick realized. A jagged spear of rock had entered her back through her spine and lodged somewhere inside her body. She wanted to touch Rick, to somehow draw off the grief and guilt she knew he felt, but didn't deserve, but she couldn't move her arms.

"Rickie fix?" she managed to say.

"Oh God, no, oh please God. Jeannie, I'm going to have to cut off your leg! Jeannie, listen. I've got to do it, or you'll die."

"Rickie, it's okay. Please just hold me. I'm already dying, Rickie. There's something in my back." She'd wanted to say "I love you, Rick" but she wasn't given the time. Her sight dimmed into blackness, and she was gone. Her last thought was that were a whole bunch of things she had wanted to tell him but never had.

Abelard was frozen in shock. His howl of grief and sadness echoed through his level of Heaven and through all the levels beyond right on up to the top. Such sounds weren't heard in Heaven. The Proprietor detected a dissonance in the Great Harmony and sent a minion to investigate.

All was clear at once to the messenger, who returned to spin out the tale of Abelard's folly and grief. "Poor Abelard," thought the Proprietor, "to have to discover thus that all things balance in their time, that great joy begets great sadness.

"But has faithful Abelard so crossed the line?" the Proprietor mused. "He did not, after all, meddle; he merely watched. Perhaps he could learn his lesson in a less devastating manner. And we can be rid of this unseemly howling!"

The minion was sent back to Abelard who was told sternly to cease howling and resume his duties. Abelard, his forlorn eyes focusing on the messenger, had trouble focusing his thoughts. "Duties?"

"You have the fate of one dog, (domestic, house), name of Sam, to determine. He is here." And with that, the messenger departed.

Abelard looked down at what had to be a poor excuse for a dog. The animal was about the size of a turkey and solid black. Sam's eyes were black also, so you couldn't tell that he had eyes unless they caught the light, whereupon they gleamed with friendship. You could tell from his snout he was a dog, but he had this ruff behind his head, like a chow, that appeared to be out of place. Abelard thought he looked like a big chicken wearing a boa.

Abelard walked around Sam and sniffed at him. "So I've got to lay out his life and death," Abelard thought, sinking down on his great haunches and heaving a large sigh.

Then a thought occurred to him. Dogs don't have such thoughts often. Perhaps it was an inspiration. Perhaps the idea was implanted. Who knew? But he had a thought, and he guiltily looked around as if some nearby being could detect the scheme that was going through his mind. Dogs would make lousy spies. Their very natures inclined them to honesty, and even after making a mistake that wasn't their fault, dogs betrayed their own transgressions with those looks that seemed to say, "I am sooooooooo sorrrry." Abelard knew he was transgressing, but the Proprietor's minion was gone, so he was at the top of the authority chain. Abelard looked at Sam with great sympathy and respect. "Sam, here's your assignment…"

So it transpired that Sam was spirited to Earth to assume the identity of a dog that, unfortunately, had the same appearance as his heavenly guise - a big chicken in a dog suit. Sam's initial experiences on Earth are unimportant. Suffice to say he ended up lost near a shopping center, there to be found by Jeannie in April of 1999.

"Oh, poor puppy. Where's your master? Did someone leave you here? Poor baby."

Her constant cooing calmed Sam as much as Sam could be calmed. There was quite a bit of energy in that chicken body, and not an ounce of meanness. Sam used his teeth for one thing - eating. He shoved his little body up against Jeannie and looked up into her kind face, his dark eyes catching the sunlight. She was ensnared as so many kind human beings had been ensnared by those looks that only dogs can manage.

When she got home and walked in the door, Rick took a long look at Sam. "That may be the ugliest dog I've ever seen. He looks like he's wearing a fur lei."

"Oh, he's not ugly! He's sweet," Jeannie said, giving the little dog a hug.

Rick knew the signs. This dog wasn't going to the pound. "Four dogs," he thought. "A new record." But true love, the love between Jeannie and her dogs, was not to be denied. And the true love between Rick and Jeannie was not to be risked over the meaningless expense of caring for four rather than three dogs.

Sam got along amazingly well with the big dogs. It was as if the larger dogs sensed that Sam's life would be brief and tolerated his frenetic behavior.

Rick and Jeannie had no clue about Sam's fate. They merely enjoyed the dog's company, and the dog returned the favor by constantly amusing the couple. Rick thought Sam looked ridiculous in normal guise until he saw Sam soaking wet. Sam emerged from a pond after his first attempt to swim with his black fur plastered to what proved to be a very small body. Except for that ruff, which stood up like black wire brush around Sam's head. "Kind of like a halo," Rick thought between guffaws. "Honey, if we cut that ruff off, we could attach it to a drill to buff the car. Or strip paint."

"Oh stop. You'll hurt his feelings. That's all right Sam. I love you. But you do look kind of stupid all wet. Come on puppy. Let's dry you off so Daddy stops laughing at you."

Sam, of course, understood none of this. But he could tell his humans were happy, so he was happy. He was so happy he squirmed and ran around in tight circles around Jeannie, his little mouth open, white teeth shining, pink tongue hanging out.

"Sam, sit!" Jeannie-human said. Sam knew sit. He sat.

"Sam, slap five!" Jeannie-human said. Sam lifted his right front paw and brought it down on her upturned palm. He didn't know why she taught him to do this. But every time he did, Jeannie-human and Rick-human would make the laugh noise, so Sam did it because it made them happy.

"What are you going to do with him when we go backpacking?" Rick asked.

"Have the Kelches feed him when they feed the cats, I guess. Sam'll stay in the back yard 'till we get back, won't you Sam?" Jeannie said, taking his black head between her hands to ruffle his ruff.

Jeannie was on her way back from the farm about two weeks later when she noticed blood in Sam's mouth. She pulled the car off the highway to look closer. Sam's entire face was black, and the blood was almost unnoticeable when it got in his fur. On closer examination, she saw a lot of blood.

Driving on to the nearest gas station, she tried to call her vet. He was unavailable. Frantically looking through the yellow pages, she found the number for an emergency veterinary clinic. She called, was relieved to find the clinic actually open on a Sunday evening. She rushed Sam there.

The little pup had lost so much blood that he required a transfusion. The veterinarian said the dog's blood had lost the ability to clot, and the condition was so severe that they even had trouble stanching the bleeding from the pinprick made by the transfusion needle.

"What'd that cost?" Rick asked the following day.

"About $500, I don't know."

Jeannie took Sam to their regular veterinarian that day. The vet prescribed steroids to help clot Sam's blood and told Jeannie to keep him quiet. At times, Sam would be okay. At other times, for no apparent reason, he would begin bleeding through the mouth.

Rick built a cage for the little dog so he wouldn't wander through the house bleeding all over the place and so the dog would be forced to remain still and quiet. They put the cage in the back room, and Jeannie found Rick back there one evening looking at Sam, occasionally reaching down to scratch the little dog's head. Sam looked up appreciatively.

"You know, he hasn't let out a peep. They stick needles in him, pick him up, set him down, stare into his mouth, stick him in this cage. He just looks at us like he's saying, 'Whatever you guys think is the right thing to do, I'll do it. It's okay.'" Rick said.

"I know," Jeannie said. "He's got such a great attitude. I hope he'll be okay."

But Sam didn't get okay. The veterinarian wasn't sure what the problem was, but he suggested the only cure might be a bone marrow transplant and extensive hospitalization. Or continue the steroid treatment and hope the dog, with a little help, recovered on his own.

"Jeannie, I know you love this dog. I love him too. Look at him sitting there. He trusts us! But we don't have any money left. A bone marrow transplant? For a dog?"

Jeannie was something of a fanatic when it came to animals, but she could recognize reality when it came knocking. Sam was dying, and although he didn't show it, he was suffering as the disease pursued its relentless course through his little body.

Over the next couple of days, she spent a lot of time with Sam. She could see the little dog was trying gamely to survive. He'd always sit right up when she came into the room, his perky head alert, tongue hanging out, as if remaining on his best, his very best behavior would help the humans save him. Sam only knew the one trick, and sometimes he'd raise his right front paw to slap five even when Jeannie was just sitting there. Sam couldn't think of anything more to do. His human seemed so sad.

Because his human was obviously unhappy about something, it was his job to make her happy again. He sat there, shifting his weight from one paw to the other. "Hold out your hand," he thought. "I'm ready." His eagerness to please overwhelmed him; he lifted his right front paw. Jeannic started crying.

Sam waddled over to her and leaned against her leg. He felt her warm hands fondle his head, felt her nails scratch that place behind his ear. He shuddered with delight and, losing strength for even these simple acts, lay down against her ankle. Blood started seeping from the side of his mouth.

Rick was still sleeping when Jeannie came in to the bedroom the next morning. She'd gotten up before dawn as usual. She'd get up about four hours before work to give her time to walk the dogs and do household chores. Rick was used to it. He slept in; he wasn't a morning person.

His wife came into the bedroom, and Rick, trying to attain consciousness, saw tears rolling down her cheeks. "Honey, what's the matter? What happened?"

"Oh, Rick, I had Sam put to sleep this morning. It was so terrible."

Rick sat up and took his trembling wife into his arms and just hugged her for a while. "Rick, he was so brave. They were about to take him out of the room, and he was looking at me like he knew what was going to happen. He just kept looking at me, and when I reached out to him, he slapped five!"

The two lovers held one another for quite a while.

It was only a few weeks later that the yard dogs destroyed the backpacking tent, but Rick didn't say much about it. Jeannie, although recovering, was in that kind of fragile emotional state that wouldn't tolerate hard handling.

They were close enough that she could see something was bothering him. She knew what it was, and though she dearly and desperately loved to go on vacation with him and their pets, some sacrifices had to be made. "Rick, we need to talk about something."

"Hmmm?"

"I know what that tent will cost to replace, and I know Sam cost us a lot of money. Maybe we should skip Colorado this year. I wasn't going to get paid for my time off anyway, so that would give me another pay week. Maybe I can pick up some overtime."

Rick looked in somewhat stunned admiration at his wife. Jeannie didn't have much of a head for finance. In fact, Rick had her credit cards hidden in a deep, dank corner of the house where, he hoped, they would never be found except maybe by an archeologist in the distant future. He'd watched the money roll out for Sam's treatment with the same sense of foreboding felt by a man on a beach watching a tidal wave build out on the horizon.

His wife acquiring a sense of financial responsibility was something of a revelation. "I, uh, well, you're probably right. I'd have been a little worried about taking the Blazer out there anyway, with 140,000 miles on it. I think next year, we'll have a new car. We could go then, would that be okay?"

"That'd be fine," she said, walking up and wrapping her arms around him. She was feeling pretty proud of herself for having landed this guy who was so concerned about her happiness that he sometimes neglected his own.

Abelard Belasarius viewed this scene in real time with a mixture of contentment and nervousness. History had only changed a little. Two people were absent from the wilderness when a huge rock fell off a mountain. What impact could that have? One person would live longer than she would have otherwise. And save more dogs, he thought. Within the span of infinite time, that couldn't mean much, could it?

His musings were distracted by a little black shape running up and plopping down in front of him. The dog sat there expectantly, as if waiting for instructions. Abelard looked at him affectionately. "You didn't have much time on Earth, but you did well, little Sam. You'll have endless time up here." Abelard looked off into the mists where the figures of a man and a woman waited, the woman kneeling, arms outstretched. Sam went bounding toward them into the mists, the picture of eternal health.

The Proprietor looked benignly over Level: Dogs (Domestic, house) knowing that all was well. And turned to other matters.

Where Sleeping Dogs Lie

It was that feeling drivers know, real drivers, those who drive for a living or for passion. Not the wives who have to drive to the store once a week at their own convenience, or the retired man heading for a golf game two hours before tee time. But the commuters who started too late in the morning and have to fight for every car length; they knew the feeling. And the truckers, those who were on a mandated schedule to get from City A to City B no matter the weather, they knew. The mothers late for the soccer game that would not wait for their kid pool, the type A personalities who drove fast no matter how much time they had, the kid peer-pressured into driving faster than he knew how - they all knew.

And Tommy knew the feeling, driving down the interstate at over 80 mph, 25 mph over the speed limit, three points and $189 if he was caught, constantly checking his rearview mirror for those flashing lights. A simple computation would have told him he wasn't going to make it, even if he had been going 90 mph, but that didn't stop him from trying. Being put in that situation hadn't helped his mood, which already had been edgy, and which was deteriorating into ill-tempered. He'd been running late when he started, and now that ill temper was degenerating into anger. It was the "why is this guy going so slow in the left lane" kind of anger. Now that he knew there was no chance to get to the farm before dark, his already-raw nerves were being abraded down to the alarm level. Fear was right below that, because he wasn't just late for dinner, he was headed for a dance with a demon.

He hardly noticed the 80 miles of interstate. He'd driven the stretch of highway so many times it had lost its allure. He wouldn't have noticed if the Burger King at St. Clair had turned into a Wendy's. Details along the highway were irrelevant; he kept his attention on driving fast and making time.

Nevertheless, it was sunset at the interstate exit. He turned south on the state highway hoping the glow in the western sky would persist for another hour. But the orange sunset faded into red, and then lost intensity until the sky looked like it was catching the glow from a gigantic dying charcoal fire just over the horizon. Even the pavement had turned from the light cement used on the interstate to the black asphalt used on two-lane state roads. Next came the gravel of the county road, which would have shown lighter had it not been for the overhanging tree limbs that shaded out any glow from the night sky.

Out of traffic, and out of time, Tommy's anger faded to musing about his own sour fate in life, or at least his bad luck today. Feeling sorry for himself was a tonic that kept him from thinking about what lay ahead. He mused that going from interstate to state highway to county road was kind of like going from civilization into wilderness. There was I-44 through Missouri - the Billboard State - aglow with towns and advertising and vehicles going in either direction. Light from vehicles, light from street lamps, light from signs, beams of light from the small airport, diffused light from towns reflecting off the low sky. Lots of light. You wouldn't expect a demon to walk out here. Demons didn't like light.

And that's how your thoughts went when you weren't trying to think about something - right back to what you weren't trying to think about.

The black asphalt of the state highway wound south toward the Ozark forests that covered the southern portion of Crawford County. The route was darker than the white concrete of the interstate that shot straight through what seemed like one continuous retail development. The blacktop snaked from town to town with occasional houses looking like unwelcome incursions in the surrounding woods. Black hardwoods leaned over the pavement. Occasional car headlights stabbed through the resistant gloom, came toward him, blinded him, and were gone.

Where Tommy turned off onto the county road, he didn't see any cars, or any homes. It was as if some zoning board had decreed a deepening darkness away from the highway. He chuckled at the mental vision of old men lined up behind the wooden tables in the old county courthouse. "I'm sorry, Mr. Johnson, a dusk-to-dawn light at that location would exceed the light limit for that area," they would exclaim in final judgment. Except Mr. Johnson could see that the old men behind the table weren't as sorry as they said they were. They were charged by the dim forces of the forest with keeping certain parts of the county hooded from honest light. By denying Mr. Johnson his dusk-to-dawn light, they paid down whatever dark debt they owed. The wrinkled and sallow-faced old men could probably walk the woods unscathed. Strangers, on the other hand, were fair game.

His chuckling faded away with that thought. The forest closed in triumph over mangled barbed-wire fences and the corpses of abandoned homes still equipped with leaning chimneys that once warmed households and now served as cold residences for rats. The structures that survived the exodus of humans into the towns and cities were mostly hunting cabins, vacant until deer or turkey season brought the humans back for a while, but not long. Everything was dark, this far away from the fast food and fireworks signs and truck stops and traffic that was I-44.

This kind of darkness one could appreciate on a starry night with the moon in its early phase, a bright sliver in the black sky with the ghostly remainder of the orb visible next to the sliver - a perfect circle split into shine and shadow. But when clouds banked up in the sky, the dark became dense and cloying, the kind of dark that wraps itself around you until you feel blind. You look in vain for the glow of a nearby town against the low clouds, then you began to look around you for any glimmer at all. Look here! Look there! Nothing. You began to think about those things that sleep during the day and prowl at night.

This was the theme of his thoughts as he drove along the narrow county road through the deep woods until he arrived at his farm gate. The visions of black creatures padding through the dark woods ran through his mind as if they were embedded in a bad movie that never seemed to end. Outside the car, it was full dark. Tommy hadn't even come close to arriving at the gate while some illumination still clung to the sky. Plus, it was overcast, so there wasn't even the benefit of star glow. Sounds unfamiliar to his city ears filled the night - abrupt chirps and screeches, sinister rustles and groans, of oaks rubbing against beeches, or wind over stones.

A dark, druidic oak rose in black silhouette against charcoal shapes of its kin in the woods beyond. Black on black on black marched the trees into the night until all was black, as if to a final curtain. His car lights - all six of them - shone on the farm gate and its shiny chain. The silver and blue of the Masterlock reflected back. The tubular steel gate itself looked a little beaten up. The barn-red paint was beginning to flake and chip. The horizontal bars showed a deep dent where someone had tried to ram the gate down, failing probably because the gravel driveway didn't provide sufficient purchase. Wounded as it was, though, the gate still performed its purpose of blocking the road.

His task lay before him. He had to leave the car, walk to the gate, open the lock, release the chain and swing the gate open. Then he had to return to the car, drive it through the opening and stop, leave the car again, close the gate, lock it and return to the car to drive the last quarter-mile to the cabin and the warm glow of the sodium-vapor yard light. But first, he had to leave the car.

"This is so stupid. 44 years old and afraid of the dark," he thought.

He wet his lips and carefully rolled down the window. Clutched in his left hand was a 300,000 candlepower spotlight connected to the cigarette lighter. Just beyond his right hand was a .357 magnum Colt revolver. It inspired some confidence. Showing off some months ago, he had murdered a watermelon at 75 yards. He remembered the red mush inside, analytically noting the fruit pulped by the hydrostatic forces unleashed by the passage of the hollowpoint bullet. He was a dead shot with the weapon, a qualified expert.

He wondered if the thing in the woods cared.

"Light and firepower," he thought. In the back of the 4-wheel drive Blazer was one more item he had acquired when he became aware of the presence in the woods. It was advertised as a combination of German shepherd and malamute.

"Perfect," he had thought. German shepherds are known for their size, strength and their instinctive protection of man and his property. Malamutes are known for their size, strength and their instinctive dislike for other dogs. He had once surmised that whatever was out there roaming the woods was a huge dog or wolf, or maybe a pack of one or the other species. Feral dogs were not uncommon in these parts. But as time passed, he realized this was more than just an irrational fear of the dark. He also realized whatever was in the woods was no animal known to man.

Nevertheless, the little pup inspired hope. It was named Buck after Jack London's hero in "Call of the Wild." London's Buck triumphed over maltreatment, Alaskan winters, wicked men and a host of other dangers to become the leader of a wolf pack in the great northern woods. Trying to protect his doomed master, Buck had killed four hostile Indians. Buck had fought and mauled a giant Spitz to become a sled dog leader. Buck 2001 would show this coiled presence in the woods what was what and who was who.

Unfortunately, Buck 2001 had plastered himself against the far side of the Blazer, eyes wide, whimper just audible. Buck had grown up from a yapping puppy into a 120-pound, yellow blob with the face of a retriever and the disposition of a rabbit. The yellow label applied to his fur color and his character. There were only two things on earth that didn't scare Buck - Tommy and Tommy's girlfriend.

Tommy sighed. He was just stalling. All this unproductive thinking wasn't getting him through the gate. The first step was to get out of the car, walk over, unlock the chain, swing the gate open, walk back to the car. All done in the blaze of the Blazer's lights. He shined the spotlight around one more time and was rewarded with an eerie display of dancing shadows in the deep woods, capering like dervishes in some mad dance. Twigs at the ends of bare, black branches looked like elongated fingers grasping handfuls of night.

"Not helpful," he thought.

Putting down the spotlight, he picked up the pistol and opened the door. He moved quickly to the gate, padlock key in hand, alert for any movement or sound. He never saw anything. He never heard anything. But he could always feel it, sense it. It was big, it was out there, it was hungry, and it could take him out in a gulp. The lock snicked, and he pushed the gate open and half-walked, half-ran back to the truck. Inside.

Buck was whining aloud now. This was the hard part.

"I could leave the gate open, drive on down to the house," he thought, but quickly dismissed the notion. The local vandals and thieves had targeted the farm almost as soon as the partners had bought it. The intruders had left some truly uninspired, but blatantly hateful messages scrawled on the wall. He'd sleep better with the gate closed and locked; he wouldn't sleep at all with it open.

The old Blazer crunched on the gravel through the open gate and halted. This was the hard part. The narrowness of the driveway snaking between the big oaks and hickories didn't leave room for him to turn around. When he opened the gate, he could do it in the bright forward lights of the car. When he closed it, it had to be done in the dim, bloody glow of his red tail lights. Beer helped. He took a major swallow, shined the spotlight around again, picked up the pistol, and walked to the rear of the truck. Part of his past routine had been to try to cajole Buck outside to escort him to the gate, but that had ended quickly. He'd spent more time outside and less time in the friendly confines of the truck.

As soon as he gave up contact with the truck, the fear manifested itself. There was the overwhelming desire to look in every direction at once, the feeling that something was near. His eyes strained to see what they couldn't see; his ears strained to identify what seemed to be the muffled sound of a heavy paw being placed carefully on the damp leaves as powerful legs eased a large body slowly forward.

He could feel red eyes upon him. It was as if the metal, the light, the electromagnetic fields produced by the engine, whatever - something about the truck helped him hide. Away from it, he was naked, a soft piece of flesh lost in the wild where hard talons and sharp teeth ruled. He pulled the gate closed, grabbed the chain from the anchoring post and fumbled for the lock. Dropped it.

There were four padlocks on the damn chain. One was a utility company lock, one was the neighboring farmer's, one's origin was unknown and one was his. "Be calm be calm be calm." Unwelcome and unbidden, the teenage stories jumped into his mind of the hooked hand reaching for the couple necking in the back seat. Arthur C. Clarke's description of claws clicking together in an alien night joined the cascade of terrifying images.

His seemingly fingerless hands finally closed on the padlock and clicked it through the link in the chain. He jerked erect, looking everywhere. He tried desperately to control his cascading thoughts. He even closed his eyes in frustration. "Stop stop stop. Walk back to the truck. It's doing this to you. It's filling your mind with fear. Stop walk stop walk." Hyperventilating, he made it to the car door. Buck was in his seat.

"Get in the back you damn worthless dog," he shouted, angry at having to perform the task of opening the gate by himself, without dog. The aggravation with Buck displaced the fear in his mind, and suddenly, the fear was gone. He got back in the truck and drove down the driveway to his extremely well-lit farmhouse. "It'd take a half-mile of wire to light the gate," he thought. "Might be worth it. When I win the lottery, I'll do that."

He'd talked to his veterinarian, John Morgan, about Buck. "John, I saw the mother. It was shepherd, no doubt. The guy swore the father was a malamute. How come I've got an overgrown golden retriever?

"Little known fact." John smiled. "Every pup in the litter can have a different dad. The guy who sold it to you, the dad he knew about might have been a malamute. There was obviously another lover in the neighborhood. How much did you pay for him?"

"$35"

"That's not a big loss. I'll put him down for you."

"I'll let you know."

That was his macho side saying, "Ah, the dog's worthless. Put him to sleep, get another. All you lose is a year or so of training." The other side of him couldn't do anything bad to Buck. Not in a million years. Even if Cheryl would allow it.

She'd be sitting on the living room floor with Buck scrunched up next to her. "How can you say anything bad about this big old bundle of fur," she would say, and Buck would display that big, dumb dog smile and try to get even closer to her. Dogs surely thought of her as St. Cheryl of the Free Home. Her long list of adoptees had included dogs snatched from highway medians, dogs wandering around in fields, dogs facing the gas chamber in local pounds, dogs left behind by friends.

Well, his first dog had spoiled him. His mind drifted back 16 years to the only other dog he'd ever had. Zeke was a mutt, but a loyal and brave mutt. Zeke's biggest fear was that his master would leave. Two families had taken Zeke out into the farmlands of St. Charles County and abandoned him, the second time when it was 5 degrees in the middle of February. Somehow, the dog had navigated the ten miles back into town, waited for a door to open and scooted on in. One look into that forlorn dog face with the wrinkled brow, and the dog had found a home with Tommy.

But his new home was small, didn't have much of a yard. So dog and owner would take day trips to a nearby wildlife area. One time, Zeke had run and run and run until the dog ran out of the territory it knew. It was the first separation of dog and master, and Zeke had cast desperately through the woods, late at night, trying to find his human. Zeke couldn't have known that his human was searching just as desperately for the dog, but Tommy had to leave the area as midnight approached. "Poor dog probably thinks he's been dumped again," Tommy had thought.

He'd had a pretty important appointment the next day, but skipped it to go back to the wildlife area. There was Zeke, sleeping in the exact spot where he'd parked his van the night before. Zeke sat up in the front seat all the way home, trying hard not to go to sleep and lose sight of his master again.

Zeke had stayed around 14 years until the cancer got him. It was painful to watch the dog try to run, dragging his useless hind legs. He'd cradled Zeke in his arms when Morgan administered the shot, and the veterinarian left man and dog alone in the tiny back yard, the man crying unabashed into the cooling fur of his dead dog.

He'd remembered Zeke, buried in the back yard in town, when Cheryl's grandmother had died. There had been something she'd wanted to say to her grandmother, had been waiting to say it for years. He never knew what it was, but it never had gotten said. Now it was too late. To him, that represented one of the saddest events of life - putting off telling somebody something until it was too late to tell. He'd tried to comfort Cheryl.

"You know, I believe as long as you remember somebody, as long as you actively recall that person, that somebody still exists. When nobody remembers anymore, I guess that person sort of goes back into the soup of creation. But as long as you think of them, they're, like, there," he'd told her.

"I know," she said. "You think because Zeke is buried in the back, we'll never be robbed."

"Well, we've never been robbed."

"Oh, stop. That's ridiculous, and you know it. Nobody'd need home security systems anymore. Just bury your dead dog in the back yard."

"I'm not saying Zeke's still physically back there. I think he's still around in dog heaven or whatever, aware of what we're doing because we, or I, remember him. You didn't know him, but he was a great dog. But I think humans have an energy beyond that of animals. People call it a soul, or afterlife, or Patrick Swayze in 'Ghost.' I think your grandma is still up there, aware of what you wanted to tell her, even aware of what you're doing right now."

He wasn't sure how much of that he actually believed, but it had seemed to help Cheryl, so he didn't think too much more about it. The only supernatural subject that interested him at the moment was trying to figure out what was tormenting him around the farm gate. He knew one thing: it hadn't manifested itself until after Zeke had died.

Cheryl had never had any problem at the farm. She conceded she was nervous around the gate. He'd laughed. "Nervous. Right." The first time Cheryl had arrived at the farm alone, she'd got out of the car and fired her gun at all points of the compass until she was out of ammo. Armed with her big .22, she couldn't have hit the side of a barn if she was firing from inside. But it made her feel better.

And after a few trips, she could get by with a couple warning shots fired in the air. And after a few more trips, no problem. Tommy thought that probably, because Cheryl didn't have much of an imagination, the thing couldn't get to her. If she couldn't see something, it didn't exist. "What is it you see out there?" she asked.

"I don't see anything. I can feel it. And every time I get caught at that gate in the dark, I know it's stalking me. And it's learning, getting better at it. I don't know. It's like there's a huge, malevolent force out there in the woods. It gains experience. It's added eyes and ears. It's adding form. It's sucking up power. It feeds off my fear."

It was hard to admit that last part. He was, after all, the male half of this relationship. The 4-wheel-drive, construction job, gun-totin' half. But one of the characteristics of a healthy relationship is the ability to talk about subjects that would be difficult or impossible to talk about with others. One time, he told Cheryl, "I used to have this dream when I was a kid. I'd be down in the basement. My dad might be there, or my brother. And the lights would be on. Suddenly, I'd be alone, and only half the lights would be on, then only one light would be on, with me right next to it. Then all the lights would be out except the light at the top of the stairs.

"I'd make a break for the stairway, running through the dark, trying to reach the light at the top. It'd be a race to escape the darkness behind me. But I'd never make it. Something, I never could see what, would grab me from behind and haul me back down into the darkness.

"So one time when I was up in Canada, it was incredibly dark. I just started walking away from the cabin, into the pines. There were things going on all around me, insects buzzing, the wind moaning, twigs breaking. I had matches, and every once in a while, I'd check my compass so I could find my way back. Otherwise, it was totally dark. And after a while, I wasn't scared. I wasn't even, you know, edgy.

"I never had that dream again. I'm not afraid of the dark. There is actually something out there."

The call came one Saturday morning, Cheryl sobbing on the phone. "Something terrible has happened. There's been an accident, and Buck's dead," she'd cried. She'd been at the farm, and had gone to town for breakfast. Ever-faithful, ever-stupid Buck had tried to follow. The dog had trailed her truck, which must have been well out of sight, down a half mile of gravel driveway.

Buck was familiar with the driveway. But unbelievably, the dog continued to follow the truck down three miles of county road, a road the dog had only seen from the inside of cars, and then three miles down a state highway. It was a narrow, two-lane state highway, and Buck got hit on a curve at the bottom of a hill.

Whoever hit him hadn't bothered to stop. Cheryl, coming back from town, sees a big yellow dog with a teal collar lying in the ditch. "I thought, 'That looks almost like Buck,'" she cried. "I saw that collar, and I knew it was him. It was so sad; he was all alone there in the ditch. I couldn't even lift him into the truck."

When help finally arrived, there wasn't much to do. They dug a grave for Buck under an ancient oak near the farmhouse and marked it with a wooden cross. It had helped Cheryl to know her beloved dog had a comfortable, shaded place to rest. The dog always had gotten so hot in the summer. As the weeks went by, they kept the grave mowed. He'd pick up rocks here and there and brought them to the grave site to make a pile and prevent varmints from digging up the body. "Poor Buck," he thought, looking at the humble little cross. "You didn't have much of a life. Not much more than a couple of years."

He remembered walking into the living room and seeing the big blond dog lying motionless on the carpet, wide awake, but not moving so as not to disturb the two sleeping cats curled up against his side, as if the cats were his pups. He remembered those big, liquid brown eyes staring at him from just outside the campfire, eager to take the proffered dinner scrap, but afraid to get too close to the strangers at the fire. Buck would sidle toward the fire until fear won out, and the dog would retreat to a safe distance.

"I know how you felt, big fella. I know what it's like to be so scared. Poor dog."

The loss of Buck cooled any desire for another dog adoption right away, plus it was winter. It'd be hard to housebreak a young pup, so there was a tacit agreement between him and Cheryl to remain dogless until summer.

He was thinking about that on a cold January day when one of his partners called to say the water had been left on at the farmhouse, and was he going down there? "I guess so," he said with some irritation. The temperature was plummeting, and the water lines would freeze and probably break if the system wasn't drained.

"Sorry," his partner said. "It was so warm Thursday, I just forgot." Missouri weather was like that. It could be 60 degrees and sunny one day, and 5 degrees with an ice storm the next day. One travel agency's advertisement said, "Enjoy all four seasons in St. Louis this week."

He sighed. Well, if he hurried, he could get down there before dark. But the phone rang and brought news of problems at a job site. When he got out of the office, he ran into the results of what some fool driver had wrought on the highway. When he got home, he found Cheryl had cleaned the house, so he couldn't find anything. A downed power line had closed Highway 94, so he had to backtrack and take Highway D, the "long and winding road." It was 6:30 and sunset before he even got on Interstate 44.

"Damn." The only kick he got on the trip was watching his odometer tick over the 100,000-mile mark. Picking up the obligatory six-pack in St. Clair, he headed south to the farm. It was the same old story. Leave the highway, leave the light, almost like he was descending into some subsurface realm. He tried to call up his image of the old men of the zoning board, but the only image he got was of four cackling geezers with rheumy eyes and unkempt, wiry eyebrows glaring at him as if he was the token they needed to cash in to get their next meal.

He dismissed the image, wishing he had Buck to talk to. At least he could have imagined that he sicced Buck on the old men, not that Buck would have ever obeyed that command. "I actually did feel better when Buck was here," he thought, arriving at last at the red farm gate. It was warm in the Blazer, but cold and gusty outside. With the radio broken again, he could hear the whistle of the January wind knifing through the thick forest. And it was very, very dark.

Humming softly to himself, pretending he was watching the branches whip around in the gusts, he repositioned the truck to shine its lights squarely on the gate. He got out. Instantly, he knew it was out there. He wasn't even through the gate yet. A mental picture sprang into his mind of a reptilian form sliding through the woods, the only soft noises it was making masked by the groaning January wind. Its eyes unblinking, focused on the prey, a black body in a black night, about to have its way, head swaying in the night, muscles bunched and poised to strike.

Tommy unlocked the gate, swung it open, ran back to the truck. After driving through the gate, he couldn't bring himself to get out. The thing in the woods grinned, black lips pulled away from immaculate white teeth. Fear was winning.

Its prey looked jerkily around. Tommy couldn't move. "My psychiatrist, if I had a psychiatrist, would say that's a giant step backward," he thought. "But my psychiatrist doesn't have to close and lock the gate."

"Damn," he thought, picking up the revolver. Getting out of the truck, he felt a sense of hungry anticipation in the woods. Behind him. He spun around. It was still behind him. "Stop this stop this stop this. This is stupid." But the sense of menace kept growing. The lights were going out in the basement.

He moved toward the gate, got there, picked up the lock, and then the lights really did go out; something in the Blazer's electrical system failed. The car died. Darkness descended like a black hood over his head. It was as black a darkness as ever seen by any sailor who was dragged into the depths of the night sea, tangled in the rigging of his sinking ship. This was not imagination. He heard, he actually heard a howl of anticipatory glee.

"My God," he thought. "That was a real noise, not in my mind." He could hear it now, it was unmistakable, the sound of scales sliding over leaves, a hissing in the night. Looking this way and that, backed up against the gatepost, he tried to bring the gun to bear in all directions at once, but he couldn't see anything. He could hear it; he couldn't tell where, but he could hear thumps like heavy, taloned feet. The sound of the thumps came closer together as the predator accelerated toward the final, fatal spring. Now, Tommy could smell its warm, fetid breath riding on the cold wind.

His mind was filled with unspeakable dread. He fired the gun, and in the muzzle flash, the form was visible. "This is no dream; I'm dead this time," he thought. The sight of his nemesis rearing up in the night brought him a strange sort of calm. He couldn't prevent what was about to happen. He could visualize the claw coming to take him, lifting him up and carrying him toward the gaping mouth. He was standing at the bottom of the stairs, and could see his mother's hand extending out into the stairwell, outstretched and out of reach. He was being dragged back down in the basement and the unending dark. He could hear the click of teeth on teeth, the raspy in-and-out breathing of a large creature, the barking…

"Barking?"

A break in the clouds put enough starlight on the scene that he could see a big yellow dog between him and the dark form, a snarling vicious dog ready for a fight, eager for a fight. Buck stood stiff legged, teeth bared, hackles up. The thing in the night recoiled, backed off. Buck pursued, and the thing retreated further, confused, scared.

"Buck?" The man stood there, no longer afraid, listening to the uproar in the forest. He couldn't see anything, but he could hear one seriously angry dog. He also could hear the sound of a heavy body moving away, crashing into things, no longer an agile, lithe predator but a panicked bully in full flight. The sounds of the nightmare beast faded away to nothing, chased from form into formlessness by a furious dog.

Soon after that, the barking and snarling stopped, and Buck came trotting back for a big hug from his master. "This is an honest to God, warm, living breathing Buck," he thought.

But not for long. Buck began to fade. He looked up at his master as if to say, "Sorry, got to go. Like to stay. Can't." And Buck went away into the night - the now unthreatening, starry night. There were sounds, but they were only the sounds of nature, natural things; a friendly place where dogs, and even the spirits of dogs like to run.

"I'll always remember you, Buck," he called softly. He'd certainly remember that last look. To some, it might have looked like a big dumb dog smile. But it wasn't. It was a grin. It was a grin of triumph.

Black And White Dog

Spot lived in a typical suburban house outside a typical Midwestern city on a typical subdivision street. His white frame house showed not a speck of peeling paint and shone almost achingly bright in the early afternoon sunlight. The house possessed a dark, well-maintained roof and was surrounded by a lush lawn, the perfectly rectangular boundaries of which were drawn by a low, white picket fence.

Not all of the afternoon sunlight hit the house. A large, dark oak tree cast cool shade over part of the yard, including an off-white concrete walk leading to a similarly-hued sidewalk next to a black asphalt road. The walkway came off the sidewalk with exact perpendicularity, as did the asphalt driveway running beside the house and leading to a modestly spacious backyard and a detached, white frame garage with gray trim. The backyard boasted several more mature, black-barked hardwoods.

Similar suburban homesteads lined the street. Not all were white frame structures. Some boasted facades of gray fieldstone. Some were solidly constructed of charcoal-colored brick. None were too ostentatious; none were too shabby.

Spot sat on the front porch of the brightly painted home at 1118 North Benton Avenue looking like the typical family dog. He was no candidate for American Kennel Club registration. He was merely a mutt of no identifiable lineage. He possessed a nondescript white face speckled with black freckles. Black, velvet ears that might have stemmed from some beagle in the family tree hung down beside his head.

The same black-and-white color scheme spread from his front to his rear end. In the aft locale, the black specks that adorned his face became broad blotches, as if some designer had been trying to paint perfect circles on the dog but gave up when the wriggling puppy presented too challenging a canvas. Yet there on his left side was the origin of his name: a perfect black circle on a field of white fur. No other name would have fit. He was Spot.

Not that he cared much about that, sitting on the porch in a sunbeam that had managed to punch its way through the branches of the big oak. Spot knew that soon, two typical, American kids were going to get off a smelly but shiny-clean school bus that stopped right in front of his house. Spot would run out to the fence, wagging his tail furiously and running around in tight circles as the kids approached. Their mom would then appear at the front door in a crisp, print dress and clean apron with perfectly curled hairdo and smile benignly over the whole scene.

That scene would be coming up pretty quick, but not right away. What was catching Spot's attention at the moment was a kind of shimmering in the street, kind as if he were looking at a painting with a blurred square of paint in the middle. It was not only the shimmering that caught his attention; there were some mighty interesting odors wafting from that direction, and he could just barely hear some muted barking from, it seemed, a great distance away.

No human nose could have detected those odors, and no human ear could have detected those sounds. Spot could, and those sensory inputs were intriguing. Spot didn't have any experience with great distances. The area in which he had operated all his life was contained within set boundaries. He knew to venture beyond the fence was forbidden. He'd tried it before, and gotten whacked for his troubles. But the fence presented no physical barrier; nor did the sidewalk, nor did the street.

Spot shifted restlessly. This day didn't seem like other days. He'd been sitting there too long, and he was, after all, an energetic puppy. All 20 pounds of him. He focused on the shimmering and the mysterious odors and tantalizing sounds. On any other day, one of the humans in the set area would have told him to be still, to "stay." He got no such directions today. He squirmed closer to the battleship gray steps of the front porch stairs, closer until his front paws draped over the top step.

He suspected that he was being a "bad dog," yet no human voice confirmed that. His focus narrowed on the shimmering in the street. Spot wasn't consciously aware of following in the footsteps of the countless, slightly disobedient puppies that had come before him, but if he focused sufficiently on one goal, he could develop a kind of temporary tunnel vision that would allow him to be disobedient - mind over minding.

At that moment, if any human in the vicinity had looked at him, they would have seen he was ready to scamper. But none of the several human masters in the vicinity were watching, and he went!

Spot raced like a rabbit across the thick grass and sprang into the air to clear the purely decorative white fence in a single bound. He hit the ground at full speed, leaping over the sidewalk in a single stride and crossing out into the street, his little legs a blur. He was actually in mid-leap into the shimmering panel before the sound of "Spot! No!" reached those flopping ears. Too late! He was gone, through the shimmering panel that had so intrigued him and into a new world.

And what a world, Spot thought. The little dog sat there, stunned, first by the wash of new odors that flooded his nostrils and overwhelmed his olfactory machinery, and then by the cacophony of sounds that filled his ears. He had landed in a meadow of tall grass that carried the smells of green plants, yellow pollen, brown dirt and decay. His ears gathered in the sounds of the wind rustling the grass and his short fur, rubbing trees together and breaking off small twigs in the upper branches, causing them to fall to the dry, leaf-covered ground below. He heard the chirps and whistles and tweets of birds, the snort of a deer and the hum of a bee - sounds that he'd never heard before.

The dog sat there trying the categorize everything when he noticed a human house on top of the hill. This wasn't like any home he had ever seen. It wasn't white or or black or any shade thereof, didn't have a proper roof, didn't even have a yard. It was kind of a long box sitting in a field with a bunch of cars like the car that belonged to the alpha male at the white, tidy, suburban house in that world on the other side of the shimmering. These cars didn't shine in the sun. In point of fact, the sun wasn't shining anymore. Little drops of water started falling from the sky, and some of them fell on Spot. And they were cold!

So he trotted up the hill to what passed for a house and went to what he thought was the front door. He scratched at it like he'd been taught to do on command. The door opened, and there stood a human female, not too different in appearance from the one at the white, tidy house. Spot whimpered a little, though no one directed him to do that. But he was cold. "And where did you come from, little feller?" the woman asked, as if Spot could answer. Spot started to stroll into the house.

"No! What dy'a think you're doing. No dogs in the house," and the woman kicked him in the side to drive home the lesson. Spot scampered away from the offending foot, back into the spring drizzle. Confusion descended upon him. Not allowed in the house?

Then he noticed this house didn't seem to have a bottom. It was held up in the air by piles of stone. Not that Spot was an architecture critic, but he did notice that it was dry under the house. He started to trot in that direction and was greeted by an even bigger surprise. An alpha male - no human, this one - came flying from under the house, teeth bared in unmistakable attack mode. Another angry male followed, both probably five times Spot's size. The pampered little dog hadn't been trained to handle this. Deep instincts took over. The little dog went flying down the hill away from the barking, growling, threatening dogs.

The alpha male concluded his statement with a nip to Spot's rear, then strode back under the strange home. About 200 yards down the hill, Spot found a relatively dry spot under a sycamore tree in the gathering gloom of the damp night and curled into a tight little ball. He went to sleep.

It wasn't a restful sleep. Being a tired pup, Spot slept soundly for a while. Then, a "whoop whoop whoop" awakened him. Then came a snarl and a high-pitched scream, like a child's scream of joy turned bad. Spot tried to make himself even smaller than he actually was and went back to sleep. He awoke several times in the night, scared and trembling, but afraid to move.

Morning brought the blessings of the sun. Spot luxuriated in the warming beams until his stomach informed him - none too subtly - that it was time to eat. Spot looked back at the house and moved tentatively up the hill. Humans had taught him lots of tricks, but none of those would serve now. This was new territory. His instincts told him that the dogs under the house would have to accept him as a member before he could have any of the food he could smell under the trailer home. Spot moved in that direction almost on his belly, his tail between his hind legs, crawling forward in total submission.

The two big males came out from under the house, stiff legged with growled warnings in the backs of their throats. Beyond them, Spot could see a female, Her posture told him she would accept him, and his heart leaped! Ever since he had arrived in this strange land, nobody had befriended him. The weather had been cold, the night lonely and full of fear. He'd been kicked by a human and bitten by a dog. Now, friendship beckoned at last.

Spot's momentary joy was cut short when he crossed some invisible line. The two big males attacked. Spot ran for his life down the hill. When he crossed some other invisible line, the attack ceased. The two big males returned to their turf.

This was so outside Spot's life experience that he didn't have a clue about what to do next. He spent the rest of the day trying to find a route to the female that didn't intersect the two, large, perpetually angry males along the way, but the geometry didn't work out. Whatever line Spot chose between the point where he was and the point where she was, that line was crossed by another line that Spot couldn't traverse without getting killed.

The little dog's next night was worse, his hunger having become a palpable gnawing in his stomach. It was that hunger that drove him the next day to eat something strange, something that had been dead for some time. It drove him to eat grass and drink lustily from the stream. And then his protesting stomach threw up the unfamiliar, unhealthy stuff that he had eaten.

Spot looked around guiltily. Such behavior usually brought punishment. Truth be told, he would have welcomed punishment if such had been accompanied by a friendly, human face. There was none such around, and Spot spent a third lonely night in the dark, unfeeling woods. The next morning, not being completely dumb, Spot chose another direction. He had a feeling that if he didn't find salvation soon, he was going to die. Animals have a certain fatalism about such thoughts. Spot didn't want to die, but he realized that at some point, further struggle would be futile. At that point, he would lie down and accept the dark shroud as it descended upon him.

Going up the hill on the other side of the stream brought him, after a time, to another house. This structure was also beyond his experience. It was a ramshackle affair that seemed to have been thrown together at first to provide simple shelter, then added to as needed. And there was more than one house. There was the big human house, a small house, a house with a car in it, a really big house that smelled of hay and strange animals, a little house that smelled of cool water and an even smaller house that smelled of…dog.

Spot sighed. He didn't know if he had the strength to run back down the hill if he had to. He was awfully tired, and not tired in the way that ended in a deep, peaceful sleep. He was tired in the way that ended in the sleep of the endless darkness.

"Oh, Patty, look! That little black and white dog came up here."

"Jeff, I know what you're thinking. We've got two dogs, three cats, two geese, four goats and that damn, pot bellied pig Matt gave you. I will not have another animal. We can hardly afford to feed the kids."

Jeff, and Patty too, were the kind of people who would take in every stray in the world if they could, but they also recognized that they couldn't, with two kids and a third on the way. Jeff had to commute 180 miles a day just to hold down a job that would pay for their rural lifestyle. He really couldn't justify to himself giving Patty the day-to-day responsibility for yet another animal.

"Sorry pup. You gotta go. We just bought this place, and we've got a lot to do. Sorry," Jeff said. Spot looked mournfully at Jeff, but Jeff lobbed a few stones at the young dog. When one hit, Spot yelped and ran back down the hill. He made it through the next night. When he awoke the next morning, his belly was swollen and hunger covered him like his own fur. He lay there for a long time wondering in his little doggy mind if it was worth expending the energy to even get up. Then he smelled some incredibly tantalizing odors drifting down the hill.

He walked back up to the lot of many houses and saw humans all over the place. There must have been 20 or 30 of them walking around, talking, laughing…and eating!

"Jeff, that dog is back."

"Oh, Patty, I'll take care of it." But Jeff got involved in something else and forgot about running off the dog. Spot moved closer to the humans.

"Hi, little dog. What's your name," one said.

"Are you kidding? His name's Spot. What else could it be," one of the partyers observed.

And a human female knelt down in front of him. "Oh, you're hungry, aren't you. Want a hot dog?" And there, magically, in front of his nose, was this long, fresh, delicious hunk of meat enclosed in more or less fresh bread. Spot immediately illustrated from whence came the phrase, "Wolfing down your food."

"Rick, your wife is about to adopt another dog."

"No, she isn't, Jeff. She knows she can't, don't you Jeannie."

Well, of course she wasn't, not any more than she knew she couldn't adopt the three dogs they had at their home in the city. Of course, she went through the motions of taking Spot back to the neighboring trailer home, and of course she saw the big mean dogs run the little one off. And of course she continued to feed him. And of course, when Rick saw her later with the dog asleep inside her jacket, he relented and allowed her to take Spot back with her. Just so the dog could get his shots and worm treatment, of course.

Spot thought this was heaven compared with the forest. Dogs were a long way down the ancestral tree from wolves and instinctively knew that long ago they had given up their prerogative to hunt their own food and make their own way in favor of a long alliance with humankind. In a more and more crowded world, for dogs, it was find a human, or die. So Spot didn't really appreciate a human sticking needles in him, and he was a little scared by the presence of three dogs already occupying his new back yard, but enduring such things was part of the age-old partnership. But surprise surprise, the big male turned out to be friendly, the female turned out to be tolerant, and the little beagle was fun too! They played and played, ran around, barked and had a great old time getting acquainted.

What a great place, Spot thought, taking care of business during a visit to the living room.

"Goddammit! Jeannie! He's done it again. I told you this dog wasn't housebroken. For Pete's sake, we just spent $1,300 for that carpet!"

Spot knew something was amiss, but he didn't know what. This hadn't been a problem in his previous life. The emotion that emanated from Rick was not unlike the emotion that emanated from the angry male dog under the trailer home. Spot was scared. Then his goddess - Jeannie - descended the stairs and ran to him. "Oh, Spotty." Then she whacked him on his rear and carried him to the back yard. He whimpered. First he was scared, then he was hurt by the one human who had shown him only kindness. Now, all the other dogs were in, and he was out. There must be some connection with his "accident" inside.

Well, no matter; he felt safe. He wandered around the little backyard, smelling the spring flowers. He found one that smelled especially good, Actually, the enticing smell originated from directly beneath the flower. He dug a little, discovering that the soil was soft and cool. He dug a little more, and eventually had himself a pile of smelly, cool dirt in which to roll.

"Goddammit!" Spot recognized the word. Usually, it came from Rick. This time, it came from the Goddess. Spot assumed his "looking around guiltily" stance that so charmed his previous household. Not this time. "How many times do I have to tell you to stay out of the flowers. And Jeez, you're a mess," Jeannie exclaimed, and then marched back into the house without even petting him!

Spot was glad to be outside. He could tell there was a major argument going on inside. He couldn't understand it, but he could hear it. "This sad act isn't going to work, Jeannie. He pisses on the carpet, he digs up the garden. Everywhere I go, I've got dogs under foot. We've got four dogs in a 1,500-square-foot house, two more than the city allows. You know the neighbors are going to report us. You've got a choice: either find him a home, or take him to the Humane Society. One or the other," Rick said.

The argument went on for a while longer. Spot didn't understand exactly what was going on, but he heard his name often enough to comprehend that he was the subject of the sometimes heated discussion. And the tone in which his name was used didn't bode well for him. Spot was beginning to yearn for that tidy white house on that tidy street where he used to live.

It seemed like there ought to be a way back. While outside, Spot actually had heard sounds that he knew came from his old neighborhood. With his yard slightly higher than that of the home next door, Spot could see through a window into a room that contained a dark box with a shimmering glass front. One night, Spot actually saw his old neighborhood in the box. If he could get through the shimmering front, he felt he could get home. But Rick and Jeannie had no such box. Spot put his head on his paws and wondered what would happen to him next.

In another part of the city lived a man who had a darker interest in dogs. He looked out his rear window at a backyard devoid of grass where a savage-looking dog lolled in the dirt. A high, wooden fence surrounded the yard. The fence looked as if it had been thrown together in a single, drunken afternoon, but its looks belied its strength. The fence represented the second line of imprisonment for the dog. The first line was the heavy chain attached to its spiked collar.

Not that the dog's owner cared about the dog getting out, but he did care about those damned lawsuits. Spike had killed two other dogs in the area. "Not that they gave him much of a fight," his owner thought with degenerate pride. But Spike needed a little more training before he'd be ready for the big time - a $1,000 fight.

Spike hadn't started out his life with this vicious streak. He had a certain inherited dislike for other dogs, but the desire to kill other dogs literally had been hammered into him. His cruel and equally vicious owner had trained him to where Spike thought tearing other dogs apart was proper behavior. The dog had been blooded through the killing of smaller dogs staked out for him to kill. What the dog now needed, his owner thought, was some larger dogs who might put up a fight. Spike had the muscle and fang and ferocity. What he needed to develop now was technique.

Spike's owner crushed his now-empty beer can and tossed it toward the trash can. "I need four or five more dogs," he thought. He went inside and picked up the phone to call Dorothy. He didn't think his wife knew about Dorothy - little, mousy Dorothy who would do anything for him. "There's nothing so disgusting, she wouldn't do it for me," Damon would brag to his friends at the seedy bar he frequented.

"Dorothy, baby, I need you to do something for me, Hun," Damon said to her when she answered the phone.

"What's that, Sweetie?"

Sweetie. I hate that, he thought. "Honey, I need for you to adopt me a couple more dogs, maybe three."

"Damon, what do you do with all these dogs?" She asked. Damon had never told her about Spike; he didn't think she'd approve. Not that her approval mattered, but Damon needed her and a couple other friends to get the dogs he needed to train Spike. "I've told you Hon, I work with a lab. They test medicines on the dogs. They don't hurt 'em; but they pay cash for dogs."

"But, Damon…"

"Dorothy, shut up! Do we gotta have a long discussion about this? Just go to the pound and adopt a damn dog! How difficult is that? Or do you need me to lead you by the hand like the last time. Shit."

Dorothy would, in fact, do anything for Damon, though she sometimes asked herself why. So she said she'd do it and hung up the phone. Now she wondered how she was going to do it. She didn't want to go to the Humane Society again. The last time had been a little scary.

"Ms. Riddler? Ms. Dorothy Riddler," They'd asked, confirming her address and telephone number. "Ms. Riddler, our records show you've adopted three dogs in the last 18 months. Your address indicates you live in the city. We're wondering if you can provide a proper home for a those dogs, let alone a fourth dog," they'd said.

Dorothy, remembering that Damon had told her not to take any shit from these do-gooders, replied, "I don't think that's any of your business. What I'm doing is taking dogs off your hands. After I own them, that's none of your business, after that," she'd said, feeling somewhat empowered by her boldness.

"Actually, Ms. Riddler, it is our business. We could, for instance, visit your home if we had evidence animals there were being mistreated or abused. It's against state law to be wantonly cruel to animals, and you can be arrested for that and your animals seized. What would we find if we sent an investigator to your house, Ms. Riddler?"

"Like I told you, that's none of your business. I told you that," Dorothy said, feeling a little less empowered.

"Our business is finding good homes for abandoned animals. We have final approval over adoptions. We suspect you are not providing a good home for your animals, based on records that show there are three dogs at your address in the city, which is a small house on a small lot. Three dogs in such a small house is probably too many.

"And Ms. Riddler, I personally suspect that I wouldn't find any dogs at that house at this moment. I can't prove that, but I can flag your records to block any more adoptions. As of now, you are disapproved from adopting any more dogs through this organization," the Humane Society lady said.

"You can't do that! I'm going to have my boyfriend come down here, and then, then you'll see. He knows all about animals and animal law and that stuff. You'll be sorry, you'll see," Dorothy had sputtered.

"Your boyfriend. Who would that be, Ms. Riddler. I believe we would like to meet your boyfriend."

"I'm gonna tell him you said that," Dorothy was shrieking now, she knew, but she couldn't help it. She wanted to hit that self-assured woman on the other side of the counter, but she was afraid to do that. She knew Damon would; Damon had hit her often enough. "You, you bitch! I'll be back here, you wait and see, you bitch."

Dorothy stalked out of the building seething, frustrated because she didn't know what else to do to get Damon his dog. Fortunately for all the stray dogs in that region, she didn't know anything about city dog pounds staffed by low-pay municipal workers who showed up merely to put in their time. Dorothy thought all stray animals went to the Humane Society. And she didn't think Damon would accompany her back to the shelter, or else why send her by herself?

So this latest request for a dog was a real problem. The phone rang in her apartment that evening. She was afraid to answer it because it might be Damon, and what could she say to him? The phone rang maybe 20 times, then quit, only to ring again a half hour later. Dorothy sat huddled in a chair with the lights out, hoping that even if Damon drove by, he'd think no one was home.

She hardly got any sleep that night for thinking and rethinking her problem. Would Damon be coming over? What could she tell him? Could the Humane Society really investigate her? That woman had sounded like a police officer. Could she go to jail for giving those dogs to Damon? Why didn't Damon get his own dogs, and what did he do with them, really? Did she believe his story? Would Damon be coming over?

She finally drifted off to sleep after so totally reviewing the various possibilities that her mind was working like a reel-to-reel tape player, repeating the same mental dialog over and over.

And then, way too soon, the alarm clock blared through her hard-won rest to tell her that it was time to go to work. She went, feeling grimy and listless and sick and wishing some omniscient force would solve all her problems, when there it was! Right there on the office bulletin board: "Free to good home. An adorable black and white spotted young male snatched from certain death in the cruel forest. He's been nursed back to health, neutered and given all his shots. All he needs now is a place to live. Can you help?"

What could be better? She wouldn't even have to pay the fee the Humane Society charged for adoptions, the fee Damon never paid her back for, she reminded herself. She called the number on the notice and got a guy named Rick on the 5th floor. "Hi. I was calling about the dog."

"Oh, that's great. What do you need to know?"

"Well, how big is he?"

"He's about 30 pounds but will grow to about 60 pounds, we think."

Better and better. Damon said he didn't want a little dog. He said the lab needed big dogs, Especially vicious big dogs. He said they were doing tests on animal behavior for some college.

"Is he, y'know, mean?"

"Spot doesn't have a mean bone in his body, but he's a pretty good watchdog. Our other dogs taught him that. If a stranger comes by your door, he'll let you know," Rick said.

"That sound's great. When can I get him?"

"Well, there's a couple things you need to know, and we need to know. Jeannie, my wife, loves this dog. We want to be sure he's going to a good home. Do you have a fenced yard?" Rick asked.

Dorothy was somewhat taken aback. Who cares what a dog wants? Then she remembered her predicament, and said, "No, but he'll be living inside."

"I don't think that'll work. He's not quite housebroken yet, though he's working on it. I think our house is the first real house he's ever been in. But he really needs a yard."

Dorothy was thinking as fast as she could. "I've got a yard. It just isn't fenced. I'll probably set up one of those, y'know, runs. That thing with the wire that lets the dog run back and forth. And I bet my nephews will love taking him to the park for, like, walks, y'know. My nephews love dogs, "she said. Her nephews actually did love dogs; they kept asking her why she didn't keep any of the dogs she brought home.

"Let me talk to Jeannie. She's gong to make the final decision. Give me your number, and I'll call you back," Rick said.

Dorothy said okay, but was a little confused. I thought I was helping him out, she thought to herself. I feel like I'm applying for a damn job or something. Crap. Dorothy eventually found out if she kept talking about how cute the dog was and how she'd always wanted one but couldn't when she was a kid and all that nonsense, this guy Rick eventually became convinced. If Jeannie had been asking the questions, Dorothy probably wouldn't have passed the test.

But Rick was eager to cut the dog population in the house back down to three, and though he thought the not-so-little-anymore black and white dog was cute and friendly, Spot still peed every time Rick came near. So Rick had given up on him as a pet and wanted to get the dog out of Jeannie's life as soon as possible. She'd gotten too attached to the dog already.

Spot knew something was amiss in this otherwise happy household, and he knew through some sort of canine sense that he was the cause. He looked longingly at the other dogs - Rex and Nikki and Jake - wishing he wasn't the odd dog out. He was really wishing he hadn't been disobedient and run through that shimmering plate in front of his too neat house on his too neat street. Spot would go back there right now if he could find a way.

But this house didn't have one of those flat, shimmering, glassy plates. For Spot, those items had a distinctive look, a distinctive sound, a distinctive smell. The more Spot could feel his time running out at this house, the more time he'd spent wandering around from room to room looking for the box with the glassy plate. With no luck.

Spot knew when the time had come for him to leave, and he mournfully sniffed at the other three dogs that afternoon. Rex, the big, strong, fearsome-looking brute that allowed Spot to win tug-a-wars, whined softly when Rick came to take the black and white dog away.

Then Rick did something he'd never done before with Spot. He set the dog down and put his arm around him, and said, "I'm sorry, Spotty. If we had a 100 acres or a farm where we could all live, we'd keep you. But this little yard isn't good for you or the other dogs. You're going to get one master who'll love you and not have to split her time up among four dogs. She'll love you, and you'll love her, and in no time at all, you'll forget about us."

Spot, of course, had no idea what Rick was saying, but the man was petting him and absently scratching his ears and being affectionate as he never had been before. And Spot knew from his scent that Rick was a good human. The dog nuzzled the man's leg as if to say, "I'm not mad, or scared any more. I'm just a dog, and I'll do what you tell me to do."

Spot's parting with Jeannie was worse. She'd prepared a laundry basket lined with his favorite blanket, a bag filled with old toys and bones contributed by the other dogs, some special dog food and treats along with brochures for Dorothy explaining how to care for and train new pets. That final scene would live in Rick's memory for the rest of his life. There was Spot, straining at the end of the leash that Rick held, trying to get back to Jeannie. And there was Jeannie, kneeling on the front lawn, sobbing uncontrollably. She told Spot to be a good dog and try to learn not to pee in the house and assured Spotty that Dorothy would be a good owner for him.

Rick finally lifted Spot up and put him in the car. Spot immediately smashed his nose up against the car window so as not to lose sight of Jeannie until the last possible moment.

When she dwindled in his sight and then disappeared, Spot's sadness deepened. Ever since his rash jump through the shimmering plate, he had been rejected by canines and humans alike. The dogs at the square house had attacked him, things in the woods had hunted him, people at the lot of many houses had thrown stones at him. Now, he had been torn away from the one human in this world who had shown him true kindness and love. He had no idea where he was headed next, but his dog sense told him he would never see Jeannie again or draw in her sweet scent. He sat down in the car seat and moaned aloud.

Rick was feeling pretty bad about Spot's situation and life in general when he arrived at Dorothy's. He had enough talent to be one of those hard-driving yuppies. If he really put his mind to it, he could make a lot of money and get Jeannie that farm. Jeff did it, and Jeff didn't make a ton of money. But Rick couldn't accomplish that today. He'd just have to try and make sure this never happened again.

Rick took Spot up to the door, and Dorothy invited them both in. Rick showed her all the paraphernalia Jeannie had provided, and then the handover was about finished. About to walk out the door, Rick turned to Dorothy and said, "I really hope you're going to give this dog a good home, because I'm married to one fine lady who will beat you with a shovel if you're cruel to this dog."

Dorothy, who was none too brave in any situation, was stunned. Rick had been so nice and polite up to that point. At first, she thought he was joking. But after further examination of his expression, she knew he wasn't.

"I wouldn't do anything to that pup. He's adorable! He's more lovable in person than in that picture you took," she stammered.

So he left. And as if the spoken word could somehow bind the speaker, Dorothy found that the more time she spent with the dog, the more she meant what she had said to Rick. The dog was adorable. Of course, those feelings she was having for the dog weren't going to change anything when Damon came knocking. Best not to get too attached to the pup.

Spot moped around Dorothy's house for a while. This place didn't look all that different from his home beyond the shimmering. He missed Jeannie's presence terribly, but dogs recover quickly from pain, be it physical or mental. At least he didn't have to keep looking over his shoulder to make sure he didn't violate Nikki's rules. Nikki was boss dog in Rick and Jeannie's yard, and had made it clear she tolerated Spot only because Rick and Jeannie wanted it so. Nikki had bright, white teeth and a no-nonsense disposition. Spot had learned her rules a lot faster than he had learned Rick's rules. At Dorothy's, there were no other dogs, no pecking order.

And as much as Dorothy wanted to keep the dog at arm's length, what could she do when the little dog came over while she was washing dishes, leaned against her leg and looked up at her with those bright eyes and white lashes?

Spot's mood improved over the next few days until Damon dropped by. It didn't require three seconds of Spot's time to dislike the man's scent. Spot detected not only the scent of another, unnaturally twisted dog, but also the scents of blood and violent death, the lingering odors of gentle dogs perishing in betrayal, anguish, pain and despair.

Humans can't imagine a sense of smell a thousand times more sensitive than their own; humans can't fathom a sense of hearing orders of magnitude more acute than their own. A dog's eyes are clear, their brains are unaffected by societal nonsense. Dogs can judge humans unswayed by such irrelevancies as skin color, beauty, neatness of dress or purity of language. To Spot, Damon wore the advertisement of his character like a broad sash of demerit badges across his chest.

The dog growled a warning for Damon to stay away from his new mistress, though she had only been such for a couple of weeks. But with Damon, Spot would have growled if he had been protecting a rabbit he had been chasing minutes before. Dogs know the difference between good and bad.

Damon only laughed. "I like him! He's just what I'm looking for. but he needs to grow a little, What is he, 40 pounds? From the look of those paws, he'll go 60 or 70. You done good, Honey. We'll wait while he chunks up a little. C'mere Sweetgums. I'll give you a taste of how happy I am wit what you done."

Spot growled again, but this time with some uncertainty as the two clinched. He retreated to a room that had been designated as his and jumped into Jeannie's laundry basket. He couldn't understand his mistress coupling with such a man, but he could stay as far away from it as he could. One thing he'd learned since jumping through the shimmering; if you rolled in carrion, you picked up the smell.

Spot would have enjoyed the ensuing weeks had Damon not been part of the unraveling tapestry. The man prodded and poked him, picked him up, peeled his lips back to look at his teeth. Spot objected, but Dorothy sternly told him "No!" when he growled at Damon. Spot didn't take it any further because he had become very obedient as he grew up.

In this life, it only required a few whacks to bring him into line. Whacks on the butt were also foreign to him, as were many other things in this reality. He knew he couldn't pee or poop indoors, he couldn't jump on any furniture unless invited, he should come when he was called, and sit when told.

And he couldn't go upstairs, although it was cooler up there, and that was where Dorothy slept. He wanted to be near her. As Rick had said, the memory of Jeannie had faded, and Spot was bonding with Dorothy. And there was a mystery up there. Dorothy would go to her room, and Spot would hear other voices, although he knew Dorothy was the only human up there. He eventually put the "other voices" down to some indecipherable human phenomenon. Humans had many. Spot was still working on the concept of a door. At one moment, there was an impassable wall; the next moment, there was a hole in it. He couldn't figure out how to make the hole; only humans could.

And there were other barriers, such as the invisible barrier at the bottom of the stairs. That was where Spot was to stay while Dorothy slept, or while Dorothy and Damon slept. Having learned the price of disobedience - separation from the gentle Jeannie - Spot slept at the bottom of the stairs until Dorothy came down in the morning.

Spot would have settled into this pleasant routine had it not been for the sense of unease regarding Damon. Dorothy was of a similar disposition.

Of all the dogs she had acquired for Damon, Spot was the one she liked the most. She almost could tell herself that she loved the mutt. She'd seen it scores of times, but she couldn't help giggling out loud when she saw Spot try to wag his tail and wag his whole rear assembly instead. The more she giggled, the more excited he got, and the faster the butt went back and forth until it seemed like his whole rear end was in a mad dance while his front end stood almost still.

Dorothy didn't live in the best neighborhood in the city. At times, she would wake in the middle of the night, oblivious to what was going on outside, to hear Spot snarling ferociously at the front the door. "I wouldn't break into this house if I heard that," she would think.

Or she'd wake up in the morning, walk out of her bedroom and see Spot doing sentry duty at the bottom of the stairs. "Anybody coming after me would have to go through 60 pounds of trouble," she thought, and gasped. "60 pounds. Oh no, Damon will be coming for him!"

It wasn't two days later that Damon phoned and announced that he would be coming for the dog. "Kiss the little bastard goodbye, Sweetcheeks. He's going to do his duty for dog and country. Dog and country! Get it? Hahahahahahah," Damon had said on the phone.

Dorothy became desperate. She realized she didn't want to give Spot up to some lab, but she didn't know what to do. If she hid the dog, claimed it had run away, she'd get a beating. And Damon would find out eventually, and she'd get a worse beating. Whattodowhattodowhattodo, she thought. Maybe I should call Rick. Too late; Damon was on his way. The police? Damon would see them and stay away. Then he'd come back and probably kill her. Damon didn't like the police.

Then her time ran out; Damon was at the door. She tried to stand up to him, a 130-pound, out-of-shape woman up against a 240-pound, fat man. "Damon, listen to me. I wanna keep Spot. I'll get you another dog, listen, please," she cried. "I will get you another dog. I want to keep this one!"

"Sure you do Dorothy, except you can't. So give it a rest, Will ya?"

Dorothy ran between Damon and the cringing dog. "I mean it, Damon. I want to keep this dog. You got to choose between this dog and me." There. She'd said it. And that was the way, she realized, that she truly felt. She didn't need or want Damon any more.

"Right, Dorothy," Damon said, and slapped her against the side of her head so hard that she fell to the living room floor.

She screamed in pain and desperation. "Oh, run Spot. Upstairs. Run!"

She didn't know why she said upstairs, except that was the room in the house furthest from Damon. And Spot knew what "upstairs" was; that was where he wasn't supposed to go. But his natural resistance to disobeying Dorothy was countered by the threat of the big, sweaty man clutching at him. Spot easily eluded those hands and ran to stand in front of Dorothy, terribly frightened but knowing his duty.

Then Dorothy made an elemental decision between her safety and the dog's. She hit Spot as hard as she could in the side and yelled, "Upstairs, run. Run, Spot!" Spot ran, past the approaching Damon, who responded to Dorothy's betrayal with a vicious kick to her ribs that left her breathless and sobbing in pain.

Spot, at the foot of the stairs, looked back. Had it not been for her hitting him - not some friendly whack on the butt, but a painful blow - he would have returned to defend Dorothy. Now he was confused. Perhaps there were two enemies in the room. Perhaps Damon's badness had merged with Dorothy's goodness, as their scents did when they coupled. "Run!" Dorothy moaned.

That decided it. Spot ran up the stairs. Damon, drunk and wheezing after the exertion of pounding on someone, clomped hurriedly up the stairs after the dog, grasping the handrail as he went to help haul his bulk up the incline. In testament to alcohol's effect on eye-hand coordination, his final swipe at the top newel post missed by an inch, and Damon, overbalanced backward, fell down the hard oak stairs. He came to rest at the bottom, badly hurt but still conscious. All he could do though, was lie there paralyzed as he would be for the rest of his life, only able to vent his rage by spewing a stream of obscenities and spittle through the hole that was his mouth.

Spot didn't know he was safe. He only knew the way back down the stairs was blocked. Instead, Spot ran into Dorothy's bedroom where the first thing he saw was the unmistakable shimmering in front of the shiny plate attached to a dark box. He hadn't seen one of those during his entire sojourn into this terrifying world. But he knew what to do. He leaped directly into the shimmering.

"Well, look who's here," said a familiar voice to the diminutive, black and white puppy with a large black spot on his side. Warm, friendly hands picked up Spot, who was back to his squirmy, cute-as-a-puppy weight of 20 pounds. "And what a mess you are," the voice said, handing Spot to one of two youngsters, both attired in striped, black and white T-shirts and stiff denims of the kind that kids wore in the 1950s.

"Yep, time for a bath, Spot. Maybe this will teach you not to go running off out of the yard," said the stereotypical mother in front of her two giggling, perfect children. A happily struggling dog, looking somewhat like a souped up perpetual motion machine, was plunged into the white suds of the gray tub out in the dark grass of the yard as music came from somewhere off-screen and the closing credits rolled over the whole tableau.

Spot squirmed ecstatically in the arms of the laughing youngster, photogenic as ever and fated to live in this happy realm as long as electronic images could be saved.

Yellow Dog

"What's the matter, McWhorter? You look like a car just ran over your foot."

McWhorter looked at George Richardson, the special projects editor for the newspaper. "I didn't get the nightside police beat job, Mr. Richardson. And I didn't get that features job six months ago. I'm going to be stuck on obits and rewrites forever."

Richardson knew a little about that. Despite being one of the most competent editors on the staff - and he knew he was - Richardson had been stuck in zones layout for seven years. He might have gotten out of there before the paper changed managing editors, but he had this bad habit of expressing his opinion about incompetent colleagues. Telling one of his superiors that working at the paper was like being trapped inside a Dilbert cartoon hadn't helped.

But the business was in his blood, and part of the mission of improving the business was identifying and encouraging young talent. "Considering the fact that you're, what?, 24 years old, 'forever' might mean six more months. Instead of crying on your desk blotter, why don't you go out and dig up a police beat story on your own time? Show somebody what you can do," Richardson said to the aspiring reporter.

"I don't know where to look."

Richardson regarded the reporter for a moment, thinking that comment sounded like that of so many reporters who needed stories handed to them. Richardson looked around the newsroom and saw too many of the staff sitting at their desks, reading or on the phone. They should get out of the office once in a while, he thought. And he wondered if McWhorter was the type that never left the building, the type that had no instinct for a story.

If he was, Richardson didn't have time for him. "Then again, there's always the possibility management was right about you, that you belong on the obit and rewrite desk," Richardson told him.

Richardson's bluntness startled McWhorter. Most of the politically-correct editors around this newspaper avoided any kind of criticism, even constructive criticism, especially to people like McWhorter, a slim, almost effeminate looking black man who had gone through school on a minority scholarship. The Post, after awarding him the scholarship, almost felt compelled to hire him after graduation. Many reporters who got into the business by more traditional means tended to look down on him for that reason. Maybe the editors in charge of promotion did too.

McWhorter knew Richardson wasn't that type. Richardson didn't care about anything except putting out a good paper. He was a middle-aged, white liberal who had been in the business for 30 years. He and his wife had adopted one child from China and one from Sierra Leone. If Richardson was chastising McWhorter for whining, then it was because McWhorter was whining.

"You're right, Mr. Richardson. I'm 24. I've been out of college for three years and worked here for one year. Maybe you could, like, point me in the right direction. I can take it from there. I just have a little trouble figuring out where I'm going to find a good story on my beat."

"Fair enough," Richardson said. "Rewrites probably are a dead end. The editors have already looked at them. Let's look at the obits. You write 'em. There's probably a story behind one of those deaths, or a story of the lives before those deaths. It's not just celebrities who lead interesting lives. Many of us do. Look for the unusual, McWhorter, Make a few phone calls, do a little legwork. Tell me this afternoon if you come up with anything."

With that, Richardson went back to his own work. McWhorter wasn't one of his reporters, but the veteran editor couldn't help giving advice when honestly asked.

McWhorter, recognizing dismissal, returned to his desk and started reading the obits of the last few days. He hadn't realized it, but he'd been writing the things so mechanically, he didn't remember doing half of them. They all sounded alike. All done in the precise Post style, all very formulaic, all very correct, all very boring. After a hour or so of reading them for content, he realized these articles wouldn't impress anyone with his writing talents. They didn't impress him, and he wrote them.

Wait a minute, he thought. Here's something.

Funeral services for Alexander Emmanuel Cotten will be held at 3 p.m. at the Smith-Thompson-Edgar-Byrnes Funeral Home, 420 North 6th Street, Clayton. Visitation will be from 9 a.m. to 3 p.m. at the funeral home. Burial will be at 6 p.m. at Clayton Memorial Gardens, 1856 Clayton Road.

Mr. Cotten died Tuesday (Jan. 3) of as yet undetermined causes. He was 47.

Mr. Cotten was active for 15 years in the Clayton Jaycees. He had held several offices with that organization, including chapter president. He later advanced to become a state director and state president. The Clayton Jaycees gave a JCI Senatorship - the highest award a Jaycee chapter can give - to Mr. Cotten in 1997. Under the leadership of Mr. Cotten and his successors, the Clayton group became the largest Jaycee chapter in Missouri.

Mr. Cotten was a CPA with Barnes & Worthington of Richmond Heights.

He is survived by his wife, Alicia Cotten of the home; his parents, Thomas and Jean Cotten of Asheville, N.C.; and a brother, Thomas Jr., of Golden, Colo.

Memorials can be made to the Clayton Jaycees.

Cause of death undetermined, thought McWhorter. Here's a guy, 47 years old, lives in a nice town, good job…If the cause of death was cancer or heart failure, we'd have said that. So it's probably a suicide. I'll just ask his wife. Then he groaned inwardly. How do you do that? Do you just ring the doorbell and when she comes to the door say, "So, did your husband off himself, or what?"

Darryl almost picked up the phone to call Alicia Cotten, but remembered Richardson going off on some reporter who couldn't identify a picture of a source the reporter had been working with for a year. "How could you be quoting a guy for a year without ever having met him? You come into the office every day, stick the goddamn phone in your ear, never get off your dead ass and think you're a hotshot reporter. Go find out if this picture is Allan Templeton, and do it in 10 minutes," Richardson told the reporter.

McWhorter, not wanting to be on the receiving end of one of those tongue lashings, waited until the end of his shift, got his coat, got his car, and drove out to Clayton to meet Mrs. Cotten. After the usual pleasantries, McWhorter ran out of things to say other than asking what the cause of death was. He was having a hard time getting that question out in the presence of a grieving wife. What if it was suicide? How do you make the transition from talking about the weather into that sore subject. There was a moment of embarrassed silence before Alicia Cotten saved him.

"You have some questions about my husband's death, Mr. McWhorter?" she asked.

"I, uh, yes. I was curious about the cause of death, a young man like that…Ah, we didn't get that information from the funeral home," McWhorter said, trying to sound like a seasoned reporter but feeling like a clumsy buffoon.

"He died of exhaustion, they think. I think," Mrs. Cotten said.

McWhorter didn't know exactly how to follow up on that. "Like, a heart attack?" he asked.

Alicia Cotten sighed. "Look, Mr. McWhorten…"

"McWhorter."

"Mr. McWhorter, my husband wasn't one to dance around a subject. I'm not either. There's a story here, and I don't think there's a chance in hell you or your paper will believe what I have to tell you. But I loved my husband dearly, and I'd like his story to be told. You seem like a nice enough young man, and I'm no writer. I have a copy of my husband's journal, the one he started keeping when all the craziness started.

"It tells his story. Take it home, Read it. See what you think. Then maybe we'll talk further. But you can only take it on the condition you promise, in writing, not to do anything with it until you get written permission from me. I won't see Alex held up to ridicule in some supermarket tabloid. I know a little about the newspaper business. I know you could get paid a lot by the World or one of those others. I won't have that, Mr. McWhorter. Do we have an agreement?"

As it would have with any reporter, that kind of proposition piqued his curiosity. What did he have to lose? He could read the journal, and if there was nothing there, just bring it back. If there was something there, the negotiations would begin.

"That's acceptable to me," McWhorter said They exchanged meaningless conversation for a little while longer, then McWhorter took his leave, carrying the thick journal with him. It was a sheaf of papers in a three-ring binder, clearly copies made from an original bound book, one of those journals or diaries anyone could buy in the stationary sections. He could see that from the lighter type near the inside edges that the copies had been made by pressing the book down on a flatbed copier. Mrs. Cotten had evidently been planning to do something with the journal, maybe try to get it published. McWhorter decided to stop speculating and start reading. He opened the book at random.

I was back in the home of my parents, the home in Milwaukee, not the one in North Carolina. Alicia's never seen this house. It's a typical ranch style, suburban home with a kitchen next to a living room next to a hallway and the bedrooms. It was perfect reconstruction, not a detail wrong. Were I still a youth, it would have fooled me. I would have been convinced it was the real thing. However, having been at this for several years now, I detected something amiss. Perhaps it was the absence of other people, family. Maybe it was some error that I unconsciously noted. I don't know, but something was amiss.

I wasn't nervous, though, because all the lights were on. Usually in this situation, there is only one weak light. My attention gets focused on that one light because if it goes out, I'm in deep trouble, I'm in the dark. And not an ordinary dark. It's a total darkness in a confined area, an area you know for certain is occupied by you and another. The other can see in the dark; you can't. The other is closing in on you like an approaching needle aimed at your eye. You know it's coming...

But all the lights were on, and that almost fooled me. If it's dark, they can come at me from all directions. In the light, I can face them and usually win. In the dark, my own fears come to their aid. I moved carefully from the living room to the kitchen. One sure way to find out if this was a real house or a battleground was to try to turn on an additional light. They don't like to concede to their foes any more power than their foes already have, and they don't like light.

I moved carefully from the living room to the kitchen and reached around the corner to flip the switch. The switch was where it ought to be, but the light didn't go on. Could be burned out, I thought, still confused about whether this was reality or dreamscape. I kept my eye on the lights in the living room and sidled toward the bathroom. It was an unusual bathroom, a rectangular room next to the kitchen with a door at either end. They'd even got that architectural oddity correct.

But the bathroom light didn't work either. It was then that the Other Siders gave up pretense and began forcing the door at the north end of the bathroom. It was a wooden door, but it bulged in as if it was made of thick rubber. Realizing that was the portal, I leaped to the door to try to hold it closed. Too late! Having gotten it partly open, it seemed as if a terrible strength on the other side was matched against my puny efforts on our side. I felt like I was trying to stop a dump truck from rolling down a 10 percent grade.

Nevertheless, I shoved hard against it, having achieved some traction on the floor. I pushed as hard as I could for what seemed like minutes, but I made absolutely no progress against the huge force overmatching me from the other side. I could feel the sense of anticipation on the other side, and fear filled me as I realized what such strength could do to a soft human body.

The matter was close to all over when the yellow dog came ambling into the bathroom as if nothing in the universe was amiss. He saved me, us, again. The dog looked like a big, blond galoot, but he is Galahad.

The Other Siders can't compete with the yellow dog. There's some purity of purpose in these animals that are fittingly called Man's Best Friend. The door shut with a decisive click, and the portal was closed. I was awake. It's 3:15 a.m., and it looked like I could get some real sleep before work.

Darryl put the journal down. What the hell was this? Was Cotten a science fiction writer or a Stephen King wannabe? The episode gave him the shivers. It sounded not unlike a dream McWhorter himself might have had. It seemed eerily familiar, the bright room suddenly going dark, inimical monsters inches away but hidden, physical laws gone awry. Yet it was written as if Cotten was in some control of the dream, as if he had some purpose. He read several more passages before drifting off to sleep himself.

He went to work the next day thinking this was too weird to take to Richardson. The editor would just tell him to drop it or make some snide comment about not having to go looking for nut cases when there were so many of them holding public office. McWhorter felt as if he ought to drop this particular project, but something about it intrigued him. If he went to Richardson now, the editor would just ask him a bunch of questions he couldn't answer.

"Well, stupid, what would those questions be?" Darryl said to himself. The first one would be: Did you read the whole journal? No? Then go read it.

So McWhorter spent the next few days reading the whole journal, all 960 pages of it. In the beginning, the journal described a young man beset by awful, terrible, debilitating nightmares that were threatening his mental health. Cotten wrote about dreams that cast him into such states of depression that some days he couldn't persuade himself to get out of bed.

When night came, anxiety about what nightmares awaited him kept him awake until the early hours of the morning.

What McWhorter found interesting was that Cotten never entertained the thought that he might be going insane. Rather, the tone of the writing was that of an athlete who was not reaching his potential. Or worse, an athlete who had reached his potential and found it was not good enough. For Cotten, the journal represented a form of self-analysis, a review of how he had performed and what he might have done differently.

Then Cotten's attitude changed. He began to write about achieving some control in his dreams, and he started referring to the nightmares as "situations," as if two opposing sides were playing some terrible war game. And death was possible. Cotten went to his death many times:

I never have to flee on foot anymore, which is good. Too many times, I felt as if I was slogging through sticky, clinging mud and the Other Siders were running on pavement. Most of the time now, I can call Motorcycle, and Motorcycle comes to carry me away if I need to run. I suppose I am dredging up memories of when I actually had a motorcycle, but these are the weapons and tools I have. I suspect a younger man without a lot of life experiences, such as motocross racing, would be at a disadvantage in this realm.

Although there are no certainties here. I have to stay aware of every detail, remain on top of the situation every second. Last night, I forgot their control of the landscape. I had summoned Motorcycle and had ridden safely away, intent upon riding around to their flank. The path before me suddenly ended. I had ridden Motorcycle off a sheer cliff, a precipice so high that the lake toward which I was plummeting appeared to be a small pond, a puddle. The duration of my descent gave me time to think that this time, this was real, and I was going to die.

I suppose if I actually convinced myself of that, I might die for real. This time, I fell for so long that I awoke before I hit. I don't know if the Other Siders came through the portal. There must be others, like me, holding the portals closed. If I were the only guardian, they would have long since entered and done whatever they intend to do to this side.

Experience tells me I fail more often than I succeed, so logic tells me there must be other guardians, other lines of defense. Or maybe the Other Siders get through now and then. Maybe they become the Hitlers and the Pol Pots and the Timothy McVeighs of the world. Of course, there was a time when I never succeeded, never won. I have, of a certainty, become better equipped, with Motorcycle and the yellow dog. Especially the yellow dog. His power over the Other Siders is absolute. I certainly am becoming stronger. You try pushing on a door as heavy as a dump truck for several minutes, and see if you don't get a workout. Then, I realize it's 4 a.m. I need to get some sleep.

Those kinds of entries left Darryl wondering if Cotten had shared these illusions, or delusions, with his wife. Naturally, Alicia had read the journals. But had they discussed this further. "And let me ask myself something else," Darryl asked himself. "Is this worth pursuing?" Would the newspaper be interested in the ramblings of a dead nut case? He needed to talk to Alicia again. And he wanted to talk to her again. She was damned good looking, even if she was 20 years older than him. And there might be something in the Jaycee angle that the newspaper could use. He was on his way out of the office when his boss, Tim Dine, asked him where he was going.

"I've got an interview at 3. I was just on my way there," McWhorter responded.

"An interview for what? You write obits. Those people are dead. They aren't usually available for interviews," Dine said, laughing at his own joke.

I hate people who laugh at their own jokes, Darryl thought, but said, "I'm working on a follow-up about a guy who died three weeks ago, Tim. He was real active in the Jaycees, and there might be a good feature there."

"I didn't assign that," Dine observed, hands on hips, chin up in the classic Authority Stance, but the effect was lost due to a zipper at half mast.

"I know you didn't, Tim. I just think it would make a good story, so I was doing it on my own."

"Then you can do it on your own time. I've got two obits here, and zones needs help with four more. That should take you to the end of your shift. And in the future, when you've got some freelance project going, don't use office time and office equipment to do it," Dine ordered.

"It wasn't a freelance job. It's for the paper," McWhorter said.

"Sure it was. And the operative verb here is 'was.' We hired you to do your job, not someone else's," Dine said, ending the discussion by walking away.

McWhorter called Alicia Cotten to cancel the appointment, and she responded by saying she wouldn't be available for a few days. She clearly felt McWhorter was blowing her off. McWhorter decided not to be put off, and ambushed her at her home the following Sunday. "You said yourself the paper probably wouldn't be interested in this dream thing, but I am," he told her. "Let's try to do two things at once - work on the Jaycee angle for the paper, and the dream angle to see where it goes. Deal?"

Alicia thought about that for a few moments before observing, "I guess I don't have much choice. I'd like to see my husband get credit for saving the world, and you're going to write about him raising a few thousand bucks for charity and saving a service club."

They went into the house, and McWhorter noticed a picture of Alex Cotten on the wall. What a hunk, Darryl thought. "Weight lifter?" he asked.

"Nope, never lifted weights in his life. Never played sports, never jogged, never did aerobics. He actually was kind of a skinny dude when we got married; looked like an accountant. He bulked up over the years. Didn't you read the journal?" she asked.

"Yeah, I did. Are you saying he got his workouts while he slept?"

"I slept with him. I know," Alicia said.

McWhorter didn't pursue that. "What's the yellow dog? Something from his youth?"

Alicia smiled. "Not exactly." She went and opened the back door, and through that door came bounding a huge, ungainly yellow dog. Seeing McWhorter, the dog tried to slam on the brakes, but had already hit the hardwood floor of the kitchen at a speed a highway patrolman would have described as unsafe for conditions. Inertia took over, putting the dog into a skid which took the big animal into the kitchen trash can, tipping it over and spilling garbage all over the clean floor. The dog got up looking sheepish - if a dog can look sheepish - then ambled over to smell McWhorter's face from one inch away.

The reporter, who was sitting on the couch, got a rabbit's eye view of a gigantic dog's head. That would have been scary had not the dog been so goofy looking - big, blond head, amber eyes with tan lashes, floppy ears and piebald nose that looked like it had been added to the whole canvas of the dog by three blind painters, each unaware of what the other had done.

Then Darryl noticed the jaws, backed by thick muscles on either side of his head. And the teeth, which more than adequately illustrated the term “canines.” Darryl experienced a moment of fear at the thought of what those teeth in those jaws could do were they, for instance, clamped down on the wrist the dog was examining. At that moment, the dog remembered what had transpired in the kitchen and realized there were garbage treats all over the floor, and he abandoned Darryl forthwith.

“Meet Wrecks,” Alicia said.

“Rex?”

“Wrecks. W-R-E-C-K-S. Alex’s dog. That’s the yellow dog.”

“That,” McWhorter noted, “doesn’t look like a hero in a war against monsters. That looks like a big idiot.”

Alicia laughed. “He’s a handful. Alex described him as half husky, half shepherd and half galoot.”

“Have you tried obedience school?” McWhorter asked.

“Flunked out. He’s untrainable.” Alicia divided her time between watching the big dog and examining McWhorter. Wrecks just wandered around the kitchen and living room, stopping every once in a while to perform his own examinations of McWhorter as if the first smell-down hadn’t fully registered.

Alicia sighed, as if what she was looking for hadn’t appeared. “Let’s get something straight here. I’d like my husband’s story to be told, one way or another. But I’m not part of it. I have no intention of making the TV talk show circuit to explain how Alex fought real monsters in his dreams. I know what I believe. I also know what I can’t prove. If somebody other than you calls me about this, I’ll deny it all and make you look the fool. There’s nothing in that copy I gave you that links the journal to me.”

McWhorter was a little stunned. "What do you expect me to do?" he asked.

"I don't know. Contact those paranormal people. Fictionalize him and write a best seller. Ask a doctor why a 47-year-old man in perfect health rolls over and dies of no known cause. Explain to me why this is fair," Alicia said, trying to wipe away tears with her sleeve, failing and fleeing the room, leaving Darryl speechless and the big, yellow dog looking at her point of exit with a furrowed brow, as if wondering what he'd done wrong now.

Darryl looked at the dog. He couldn't imagine this mutt being an asset to anyone. He doesn't even sit correctly. He sits with both hind legs pointed to the left instead of in line with the front legs. Wrecks decided he didn't want to follow Alicia. No sense seeking out punishment. The dog turned and looked at Darryl with that kind of "duh" look dogs can pull off so well, a kind of "so, whaddya want me to do" look, except you knew that any command you gave the dog would never penetrate that thick skull by the time you needed doing whatever it was you asked the dog to do.

Darryl wondered around the living room, waiting for Alicia to compose herself. There was a little poem written in elegant stitching, nicely framed and hanging on the wall.

"What have you wrecked today, Wrecks?

"What have you wrecked today?

"Have you got in the trash.

"Is there something you've smashed?

"It would be a great disappointment to say.

"That you've wrecked nothing today, Wrecks."

Darryl chuckled. Whoever wrote that nailed the dog. Wrecks does have a thick skull, Darryl thought. At that moment, the dog yawned widely, giving the reporter time to admire a truly magnificent set of teeth, the long white fangs being most prominent. He recalled what his dad, a farmer and avid outdoorsman, used to tell him about dogs and other beasts.

"Humans fight to the finish. That's rare in the animal world," his dad explained.

"But Dad, animals kill animals all the time," the boy had said.

"Animals kill to eat. That's different. But they fight, fight mind you, to get a mate, or to defend territory, or to protect a kill. When they fight that way, they only fight long enough to prove which one's the best. The other animal slinks away. Humans invented the fight to the death."

"So, how do I make Willy back down?" Darryl had asked.

"That old mongrel dog? Willy doesn't like you, so he shows you his fangs, skins back his lips so you can see the whole set. Growls, barks maybe. He's just showing you what he's got. In your case, that keeps you away. Fight's over."

"So how do I win the fight? Willy's got bigger teeth than me."

"Next time, go in there with a big stick. You might have to whack Willy with it a couple times to show him what it is. But you only have to do this a couple or more times, just to show him who's the boss," his dad had said.

And that's what happened. Darryl had gone into the barn with a four-foot length of oak branch. He recalled that he'd been scared of Willy. The big dog had made some pretty fearsome lunges at Darryl, but the boy had kept that stick between him and the dog. Got a few good pokes in too. Eventually, Willy got discouraged and slunk away, tail between his legs. They never got to be friends, boy and dog, but Darryl got respect when he went into the barn.

An older Darryl McWhorter looked at Wrecks and wondered if there was any Willy in that dog. Wrecks finally took McWhorter's examination as an invitation to come over to the couch. The dog had a wide, white chest that set off the blond hair around it. Has some shepherd in him too, Darryl thought, noticing the dark saddle across his back. Wrecks had heavy shoulder muscles and a big butt, which the dog proceeded to shove into McWhorter's leg. McWhorter deduced that the dog was butt-scratch positive and started digging his fingers into the area just above the tail. Wrecks swooned.

"I see you've made a friend," Alicia said, walking back into the living room. Wrecks, hearing his mistress's voice, jumped up, spun around and cleared the coffee table with one swipe of his tail.

"Dammit, Wrecks! That's it, Yer outta here. Git," and the lady of the house led the resident pet out the back door and into the yard, adding a sharp kick to the rear as Wrecks left the building.

"Does he ever get mad?" Darryl asked.

"No. He goes after other dogs sometimes, but he's just playing. He's a real problem around here. He needs to be up in Alaska somewhere, carrying a pack or towing a sled. Down here in Missouri, in this suburb, he has no way of expending all that energy," she said.

"Well, why don't you get rid of him?" Darryl asked.

"Alex wouldn't let me. Alex loves that stupid dog. Loved. Oh, damn," and she started crying again. Darryl mumbled his goodbyes and left. He went home and paged through the journal trying to find references to the yellow dog. It wasn't easy. Alex hadn't indexed anything in the journal. He barely kept track of dates. The manuscript was just one long, running account of events Alex had either experienced or imagined.

I guess I knew where I was going when I got there. There wasn't a lot of deception involved. The portal was obvious, a long tunnel, just like one would imagine it to be, a connection between Hither and Yon. Looking at what was coming down the tunnel, I tried to block it. The only thing at hand was a heavy coat, and I threw it up. The coat caught on some hooks in the tunnel, and blocked it.

The coat didn't do anything, of course. As soon as it was hanging in front of me, I knew something was directly behind it. I clenched my teeth and pulled the coat a little to the side. Shouldn't have done that. I got a view a big, hairy head with greasy, tufted ears and thick saliva dripping from its mouth. It was big, as big as a bear. I wanted to run, but you can't turn your back on the Other Siders, no matter what. We struck at one another, I with my right hand, the monster with its left. I had a feeling like I'd tried to pick up a boulder, far, far too heavy for me to lift, such was the difference in arm strength between us. The monster gripped my wrist, and I was convinced it was going to rip my arm off, so convinced that I wondered what life would be like without a right arm.

Then the bear-head's strength seemed to ebb, and mine grew. It looked at me for the first time, red eyes that had been so sure of victory moments before were now perplexed as to why its thick, heavily muscled arm was being shoved back by mine. We have a power on This Side beyond that of the Other Siders, almost as if the rules of the Universe take strength from the trespasser in proportion to their distance from their rightful home.

It takes such a terrible toll, though. I woke up feeling as if my body was a sheet of iron lying like a pancake on a powerful magnet. I couldn't hardly move, so spent was I after the stand-up arm wrestle with the beast. My antagonist had broken away and retreated down the tunnel. I did not follow. I do not know what rules apply, but it seems I would be at as great a disadvantage on the Other Side as they are here.

I think I know how this works. We stare each other down. When the Other Siders back off with their tails between their legs, we have won. When we lose, we wake up. That's the way we slink off. We wake up, beaten and discouraged and bone tired.

Darryl sat back in the chair. Alex never described much of the dog's actions. Wrecks just seemed to be either on the periphery of the dream events or outside entirely. Alex's confrontations with the Other Siders began to remind Darryl of what his father had told him about animals fighting. It seemed as if one or the other would gain the upper hand, whereupon the other would retreat. Was Wrecks the weight that swung the balance of power, or just one of Alex's "tools," like Motorcycle?

Well, he had enough on the Jaycee angle for a regular newspaper story. He even had a news hook: the Clayton Jaycees were going to petition the city council to name a street after Alex, the street where a low-cost housing project was being built. Alex Cotten had been the chairman of the committee that made the whole project possible. That was pretty impressive, Darryl thought, a chapter with 120 members - maybe 60 of them active - and about $7,000 in the bank becoming the sponsoring agency for a $3.5 million apartment complex for the elderly and disabled.

So he had that story, and it was good. I guess that's what Richardson said about knowing your sources, Darryl thought. Between Alicia, several Jaycees and a couple city council members, the story really came to life.

So, what about his other story? Darryl waiting until Richardson looked like he had a free moment and went over to talk to the editor. "Yeah,

I've got some time. Let's go down to the barfeteria and grab a bite," Richardson said.

As they sat down to eat, Richardson said, "You know, that was a pretty good job on that Cotten story. That's the kind of thing this newspaper has to do, pick up on stories that radio and TV would never get. The only way those talking heads ever get a story is if it walks in the door and pokes them in the eye. Every time we dig up something like you dug up, we increase our value to readers. In this day of spoon-fed television news, that means a lot. And I know you did that on your own time. I'm going to see if I can get you some overtime for that," Richardson concluded, looking down at his plate. "Did they say this stuff was fish?"

"Mr. Richardson, there's more to this Cotten story, but it's pretty fantastic." McWhorter then related the whole thing with the journal, the yellow dog, the monsters, Alex's theories, feeling more and more foolish the further he got into the story. He was. after all, talking to a man who'd spent decades in the nothing-but-the-facts, don't-use-it-if-you-can't-prove-it world of newspaper journalism. McWhorter was talking to a man who not only ridiculed the tabloid press, but deeply and fervently hated what such sensationalistic claptrap and outright fiction had done to the public perception of what newspapers ought to be. Richardson said tabloid journalism led to tabloid TV, and if the supermarket press was the devil's work, tabloid TV was Satan himself.

And here I am, Darryl thought, spilling out this tale of a dream gladiator protecting the world from a variety of monsters accompanied by his trusty pup, Wrecks. What was I thinking? By the time he was finished, McWhorter was ready to crawl away into some obscure corner of the newsroom and stay there for the next year or so.

Richardson surprised him. He leaned back in his chair and asked, "Do you believe it?"

McWhorter thought for a moment. "Cotten wrote about this dream where he was fishing, having a good time, when his boat suddenly sank. He was treading water next to some reeds when he spotted a big rattlesnake. Cotten tried to back away in the water, but the snake saw him and started swimming straight toward his head. Can you imagine something so horrifying as trying to swim backwards in the water and having a big pit viper arrowing right at your face? Cotten had a pie plate, or a camp plate in his hand. The snake would strike at him, and he'd stop him with the plate. So the snake divided into two, then four, then eight different snakes, all driving inward at his face. Alicia said she woke in the morning to find her husband crouched, asleep, in a corner of the bedroom, holding an Indian dream catcher in his hand. That dog, Wrecks, was sitting in front of him, wide awake, fully alert. If this wasn't reality, they certainly thought it was."

Richardson looked pensive. "I spent three years in India working for the Press Trust. I saw some things there that defied what we would call logical explanation. A story like yours, in certain places, would generate a lot of interest, maybe some explanation."

"I thought you'd ream me out," McWhorter said.

"I might have, but I've heard that story before," Richardson said. "We can't use it, of course. I don't know if you could peddle it anywhere as nonfiction. If it was me, and it was once, I'd just salt it away as one of those paranormal events that mankind won't be able to explain for a few hundred years."

"You've heard this story before?" McWhorter explained.

"Not exactly, but the gist of it was the same. You know, the practice of medicine as we know it is only about 100 years old. It wasn't all that long ago that we couldn't figure out why people got sick after drinking water downstream from where the cattle were crossing. And we know less about the human mind than we know about the human body. We're still discovering amazing new things about the earth while the Hubble telescope is bringing us new mysteries from deep space. Who's to say what's reality and what's not? Stephen Hawkins says there might be nine dimensions. I can't imagine any more than four. If you've got evidence something beyond our ken was happening with Cotten, then maybe something was. But like I said, it's not for us."

"Well, thanks for not laughing at me, Mr. Richardson."

"Call me George, next time."

On his way home that night, he stopped by Alicia Cotten's house to give her the news that the paper was going to give pretty good play to the Jaycee story. As they were talking, he heard Wrecks crying outside. He knew Alicia banished the dog to the backyard when his behavior became intolerable, which meant Wrecks spent a lot of time in the backyard. "What'd he do this time?" McWhorter asked.

"Oh, nothing. It's just every time I turn around, he's there sticking his nose into my face. He managed to walk by the bed this morning and knock out my contact lens with his tail. Then he pushed the laundry room door open and ate the cat crap, and now his breath smells just wonderful. He just drives me crazy," Alicia explained, then looked at Darryl as if she'd just gotten a bright idea. "He likes you, though."

"He likes anyone who'll scratch his butt."

"No, really, he does things with you that he used to do with Alex, that he doesn't do with anyone else. Really, I'll show you," she said, and left the room to let Wrecks in the house. Wrecks entered the house at the gallop, and, seeing McWhorter, tried to make a high-speed turn on the hardwood. The front paws held, but the hind ones lost traction, and the 120-pound dog spun out into a dining room chair that crashed into the dining room table which overturned the floral centerpiece, spilling black dirt all over the table. Alicia stood in a corner of the kitchen surveying the whole scene in much the same manner that Joan of Arc must have contemplated martyrdom. Having finished his depredations in the kitchen, Wrecks trotted over to McWhorter, who was sitting on the couch.

The dog looked at him for a moment, squirmed a little, got up, walked in a circle, sat down and put a big paw on McWhorter's knee as if to say, "Pet me, Darryl. Please. Be my friend. Please," with those big amber eyes and furrowed brow in full beg mode.

"See, with everyone else, he sidles up to you to get his butt scratched. That bit with the paw, he only did with Alex."

McWhorter looked at the yellow dog, and the yellow dog stared intently at the man. Realization hit McWhorter. "Oh no, I'm not taking this mongrel. I know a conspiracy when I see one. Thanks anyway, Alicia. I gotta go."

"Bye Darryl," Alicia said as the reporter squeezed by the dog and out the door. Wrecks ambled over to her, and she stood in the living room, absently scratching the dog's head. "It's your decision, Wrecks. I don't see it in the man, but I'm not you." She went upstairs to the bedroom, Wrecks following closely behind, almost underfoot. She went to the bedroom and pulled out Alex's journal, the whole journal, not the edited version she gave to McWhorter. She opened it to a certain page:

As soon as I walked into the house, I asked myself why I had selected this particular dog to adopt from the pound. The dog is too big for the house; indeed, he's too big for the entire block. He doesn't learn, he doesn't behave, he's annoying.

Yet every time I decide to take him back to the pound, he trots up to my chair and puts his paw on my leg as if to say, "I know I don't seem like much, but I have value, if you just believe in me. My time will come. Please don't send me away." At least that what it looked like he was saying. One reads what one wants to from a dog's expression.

So I can't bear to take him back to the pound, I couldn't live with the memory of the look he would give me as I walked away. It's hard enough to go to work and see him watching from the backyard, both feet looped over the top of the fence, watching me drive down the street, wanting to go with me. So it is left to me to decide what worth he has. Maybe he's a part of this fight against the Other Side.

Alicia sighed, and skipped to the back of the journal. She had read these passages many times, and she would read them many times again. She and Alex had had a love unusual in these times of divorce and trial separation and living together and open marriage. They had loved one another, and only one another. She was not part of his battles on the dream fields, yet felt his fatigue and pain in those terrible mornings after. She knew the part the yellow dog played, and knew that she and Wrecks would be separated. She could not take Alex's place in the great struggle, and whoever did would need the yellow dog.

She hated that. Whatever she had told McWhorter and the other candidates, Alicia loved the big cur. She felt safe around him, and all his bumbling antics made her laugh in this time of great sadness in her life. As she sat on her bed, Wrecks went over to his little basket of chew toys, knocked it over, smelled them all, picked one up and brought it to her. He looked at her expectantly. "I know this trick, Wrecks. You're saying 'I don't have much. But I'll give you this toy if you won't be mad at me.' I don't know what you did, Big Dog, but I forgive you." She scratched his butt to show him she wasn't mad any more, and picked up the journal again.

Last night, I found myself in a bar in an argument with these thugs, three or four of them. They looked like comic book villains, big, mean guys who liked to fight and hurt people. I remembered being scared, and trying to figure some way out of the situation. My companions of a moment ago were gone - humans always leave me - and I was alone with these angry, advancing goons.

I tried to fight, but I couldn't lift my arms. I had the mental toughness not to turn and run, but I was helpless, my arms at my side feeling like I had a cinder block glued to each hand. Then I felt a furry head at my side. I managed to lift my right hand to a strike a blow. The force behind the blow wouldn't have knocked over a bicycle in the real world. The thick-bodied thug went down, though, and his buddies disappeared. I kept hitting the one on the floor until he became smaller and smaller and eventually retreated through the wall. Only the yellow dog remained in the bar, looking at me, tongue hanging out, as if to say, "Nice work." I tried to reach him with my hands to fondle that big head, but I couldn't lift them. I tried to tell him "thanks" with my eyes.

On the Saturday after Alex wrote that passage, Wrecks, on the assumption the three of them were going for a ride in the car, ejected himself prematurely through the front door, out into the yard and into the street. Unable to contain his energy, Wrecks jumped up on the hood of the car and struck a pose that made him look like a grossly oversized hood ornament. That represented quite a distraction to passersby, and one driver was distracted long enough that he nearly ran into an oncoming car. That motorist swerved and rammed into Alex's stationary car with the Wrecks hood ornament. The impact sent the dog flying.

Alex and Alicia ran to where the big dog lie stunned on the ground. Alex stayed to deal with the accident and the police while Alicia rushed Wrecks to the animal hospital. He was okay, the vet said, but suggested she leave the dog overnight just to be on the safe side. Without his dream guardian, Alex died in his sleep that night. After the funeral, Alicia retreated to the journal and read Alex's last entry.

I should probably spend some time bragging about how we bricked up another portal last night, but I have this sense of doom. I hope it doesn't have anything to do with the yellow dog; I called just before the clinic closed, and they said he was fine.

Maybe this sense of doom pertains to me. I should tell Alicia that if anything happens to me, she'll have to help the yellow dog find another, and let the dog go to whomever that may be. As much as she curses and screams at the dog, I know she loves him and cherishes the aura of protection he carries with him. It is, after all, his purpose to protect those he loves.

She has been with me in these dreams. We are too close for her not to be. I have felt her presence. Or the Other Siders send copies of her to abandon me in some setting, a blatant attempt to weaken me mentally. Such stratagems merely demonstrate her worth. Alicia can't stand next to me in the fight, though, the way the yellow dog can. This struggle takes place upon some mental plain on which only a few can stand. The yellow dog is an asset we can't afford to lose, and Wrecks can only operate in tandem with one such as I.

Another thing I should tell Alicia is how much I love her...

And that was the end. She thought about how Wrecks had placed his big paw on Darryl McWhorter's knee. She shook her head slightly, still disbelieving the clear implication of that gesture but knowing what it meant: she was going to lose both the males she loved in the same year.

Across town, Darryl turned and writhed on sweat-soaked sheets. From the glimpses of memory that remained later, he had been walking down a narrow path in a dank cave, a vertical cliff on his right, and a dirty, subterranean lake on his left. As he walked, the path narrowed and began to tilt toward the black, roiling water. He could tell by the shape of the ripples that there were knots of snakes just below the surface. He couldn't retreat because of a black wall that followed in his footsteps.

Darryl tried desperately to cling to the slippery path and stay away from the water, but the black wall steadily advanced, and the trail developed a steeper and steeper incline toward the now eager water. Darryl turned and tried to push back the advancing black wall, knowing this was the entity that ought to be opposed. He didn't last long, though. He slipped and slid into the oily water. His last glimpse was of the white mouths and shining fangs of the waiting serpents.

Darryl woke from the agonizing nightmare, and there in the dark gray dawn began writing in his own journal.

Some miles away, Wrecks whimpered and put his big head on his paws. He rested in the cool grass of Alicia's backyard and waited impatiently for his new master to come for him.

Jake

It had been one of those days. First of all, the car wouldn't start. I spent about an hour trying this and that, including calling the shop and ordering a new battery, before it occurred to me to check and see if the battery cables were loose. They were. Five-minute job, and they're fixed, and I wasted an hour trying to figure out what was wrong.

Then, of course, I was late for work. I don't like my boss anyway. He's one of those people who rose through the ranks with a permanent butt print on his face. He took care of all his buddies, and gave the rest of us the shifts that were convenient only in European time zones. Needless to say, he didn't like me either; hence, the 5:30 p.m. to 12:30 a.m. shift, Tuesday through Saturday. Seems to me, that's punishment enough for 42-year-old single guy who's never been married and who ought to think about finding a spouse before he makes the turn into middle age.

He shouldn't have even been there when I arrived at 6:30ish. Evidently his boss had kept him around after 5, so he was already pretty annoyed by the time I strolled in. So he got on my case about being late, and I said this, and he said that, and I suggested that his very existence was a waste of skin, and he informed me that insubordination was an actionable offense under the union rules, and I said it was a good thing there was a union to protect us all from promotion into the levels of incompetence where he was, whereupon he said I was asking for a couple unpaid days off, so I said fine, and walked out before he could change his mind.

I didn't want to answer the phone when I got back home because my boss would just now be remembering that there were only a few other people who could do my job, and fewer who would be willing to do my job at that time of day. The union rules are that you have to give someone 12 hours notice for a shift change. If you didn't give them 12 hours notice, the boss had to beg and plead. I felt better because of that on the way home. Courtney'd have to go looking for a replacement. If he couldn't find one, he'd call looking for me. If I answered, I'd get in another big argument that actually might get me fired.

So I didn't answer the phone when it rang, just listened to the answering machine. It was my girlfriend leaving a message "that we have to talk." I don't know how much experience you've had with the fairer sex, but "fairer" doesn't refer to rules of engagement. It refers to looks. The rules change as you go along, but some things are constant. If "we have to talk," it ain't good for the guy.

It meant she'd made a decision on which of us, me or her other boyfriend (assuming there was only one) she was going to retain to make sure her future was emotionally secure. From the tone of her voice, I knew I was the dumpee, so I didn't feel like talking to her. She clearly wasn't the kind of woman - girl, actually - who would spend her life with one guy, which was what I wanted. Best to get out of these things before you get too hooked on the girl. After listening to her leave her message, I checked the mail and found a letter from the IRS saying I owed them $1,200 in interest and penalties from not declaring as income some savings bonds my aunt had left me three years ago.

That was all the news that I needed to fill my cup that particular Thursday. I headed to the bar before any more bad news could find me at home.

I didn't head to my regular bar. I didn't want to run into Tammi - the newly ex-girlfriend - and I really wasn't in the mood to run into my usual drinking partners. I was tired of their stories, and they probably were tired of mine. I'd heard about this place over on Fourth Street, so I went there. Maybe I could meet some women over there. I knew them all at the old place. What the hey. I've had disaster after disaster in the area of male-female relationships. So try someplace new. The worst that could happen was I'd meet another woman with zero capacity for real love. I mean, why is it half the married couples can stay together their whole lives, and half got two or three or more marriages under their belts? What does the first group know that the other group doesn't? Questions to ponder over a beer, I thought.

It was mid-afternoon, so there were only a couple guys there. One looked like that portable asset most small bars have, a guy on a pension who comes in at opening time every day and drinks himself into oblivion by 7 o'clock. The only cost associated with serving him is calling a taxi every night. But while the pensioner is there, he bores every walk-in to tears. He already had a victim cornered and was telling him some story about how great his life had been. I sat down at the other end of the bar and tried not to make eye contact.

"Don't sit there," the bartender said.

I looked at him with kind of a "is this some kind of joke" expression on my face. I mean, the bar had maybe twenty stools, and only three, including mine, were occupied. It had a row of four booths in which no one was sitting; a pool table at which no one was playing; a little dance floor on which no one was dancing; some video games at which no one was standing; and a couple restrooms. Unless the restrooms were occupied by 50 people about to come back and reclaim their seats, I couldn't see what the problem was.

I said, "Look, Pal, I just didn't want to intrude on that guy's life story down there. What's wrong with this stool? Is it about to buck me off or something?"

The bartender walked over and leaned on the bar. "That stool's reserved for someone who might come in here later. You ever seen 'Cheers?' That's Norm's stool. Any one of the others would be fine," he said. I would have thought that this bar's Norm was the old guy pouring out his life's tale at the other end of the bar. But who cares; I wasn't about to get in a big argument over where I was sitting in an almost empty bar. I moved down a couple stools.

"This better?" I asked.

"That's great," said the bartender. "What can I get you?"

"Beer."

"What flavor?"

"Cold. Whatever comes out of that tap," I said, and he went to fill the order.

While the bartender was doing that, the guy who'd been cornered by the old drunk broke away and came down and sat next to me. "Hey Chief," he said. "Pretend like you know me. That old fart's been bending my ear for a hour. I feel like I need to take it to a body shop."

I laughed. Maybe this guy wasn't such a schmoe. "Name's Al," I said. "That's why I sat down here. I didn't want to listen to it either." Then, for lack of anything else to say, I asked, "What's with the chair?"

"I'm Tom. You mean that chair? That's Sue's chair. Nobody sits in it. Kind of a bar tradition."

"So when does Sue come in?" I asked. "I'm between girlfriends as of this afternoon, one of about 900 reasons I'm here."

"Sue won't be coming in today. Sue won't be coming in tomorrow. Sue won't be coming in, because Sue's dead. Killed in a car accident about eight months ago," Tom said.

I chewed on that for a while. "Seems like a long time to keep a seat warm for someone who's stone, cold dead. She own the place or something?" I asked.

"Naw, she just drank here a lot. That guy," he said, pointing to the bartender, "owns the place. She was a good customer. So was her boyfriend, Ben. He was a real good customer. Used to come in here maybe three, four nights a week. After he and Sue got together, the first thing he'd do when he walked in here was look to see if she was sitting on that stool."

"And after she died?" I asked.

"The first thing he'd do when he walked in here was to see if she was sitting on that stool," Tom said, taking a drink of his beer. He looked at the ornate woodwork behind the bar for a moment, turned his head back to me. "He couldn't accept that she was dead, y'see. He kept wishing that she'd be there, like if he wished hard enough, she would be there. And if someone else was sitting there, he'd ask them to move."

"So what happened if they didn't move?"

"Ben would move them," Tom said. "Ben didn't take any crap from anyone. So Schappe" - he gestured at the bartender - "just won't let anyone sit there. Stops a lot of fights before they happen."

"So does Ben still come around here."

"Nope," said Tom. "Ben disappeared off the face of the earth about five months ago. Nobody's heard from or seen him since. Didn't quit his job, didn't sell his condo, didn't leave a note, nothing. Just vanished."

This was getting interesting. I made my living copy reading for a book publisher. I hadn't told Tom that, so he wasn't pitching me some story he was certain would be a best seller if he could just find a publisher. People do that when they find out you work for a book publisher. And I had a whole afternoon and night to waste, not having to worry about a hangover the next day. Way I saw it, the boss gave me two days off, which to me was one to get drunk and one to recover.

I mentioned that to Tom, skipping the part about where I worked, and he said, "Ben used to say stuff like that. Like, he said you shouldn't get your birthday off. You should get the day after your birthday off, to recover from your birthday party. He was hilarious. He'd sit at this end of the bar - this was before him and Sue fell in love - and just rant about anything. He was a great story teller. Half the bar would be crowded around this end listening to him yap."

"So is there some investigation about what happened to him? I didn't hear anything about this on TV," I said.

"I don't think TV ever picked up on it, don't know that they would. I think it was in the local paper that he disappeared, but the cops said there didn't seem to be any foul play - no body, no note or anything like that. They said it was 'under investigation,' which around here means that they ain't doing anything. But then again, maybe he just took off for Alaska or something. He really loved Sue, and her dying really messed him up; broke his heart, really," Tom said.

I got to asking myself whether or not Tammi broke my heart. I concluded I hadn't got that far with her, which was probably a good thing. I'd be in worse shape if I'd actually fallen in love with her, or worse yet, married her. I probably didn't know what true love was, or I'd be broken like this guy Ben was. I was getting away from Tammi before I fell that far, I decided, or maybe I just didn't want to find out what true love was. You have thoughts like that while you're swilling beer. These thoughts seem quite profound at the time you have them. Next day, you wish you hadn't shared such moronic maundering with people who might remember what you said. Good rule in a bar; keep it short.

"I think my girlfriend is going to Seattle to live with some guy on a boat. I'm so in love with her, I think I'll let her go," I commented, motioning to Schappe for another beer. I asked Tom if he wanted one. "You're telling the story. Does it have an end, or are you guys just going to sit around waiting for some dead gal to fill that seat?"

"Schappe thinks he knows how it ends, but I think Schappe's nuts. Hey, Schappe, come over here," he yelled at the bartender. "Tell this guy what happened to Ben."

Schappe looked at Tom. "What'd you tell him so far?"

"I haven't told him about Jake yet."

"Who's Jake," I asked.

"That was Sue's beagle," Schappe said. "She was a vet tech. She rescued the dog from the animal hospital where she worked. You should have seen this dog, fat little guy," Schappe said.

"He didn't start out fat," Tom added. "The dog had heart worms, first of all. Second, it was abandoned on the street."

"And it had a collapsed throat or something," Schappe added. "They brought Jake in here one afternoon. Jake would go off in the corner and cough like its lungs were coming out its mouth. The first time, I thought the damn dog was throwing up in the corner, but the cough just sounded like that. Sue's boss, the veterinarian, said the dog only had about three months to live.

"So she brought it home. Said she thought it should die in a nice place, not some cold cage in an animal hospital, all alone. She fed it milk and dog biscuits, made a little bed for it. Called him Jake. Even slept with him some nights. Well, after the mutt found himself in a nice home, good food, warm place to sleep, someone to love him, Jake perked right up."

"Yeah," said Tom. "The vet gave him three months to live. Three years later - three years! - Jake's still alive and weighing in at about twice what beagles ought to weigh."

Schappe started laughing. "Ben came in here one night a couple winters ago, and I asked, just to make conversation, 'How's Jake?' He says, 'Jake got high-centered down on the farm.'"

"High centered? I asked. 'Yeah,' he says. 'You know that snow we got. It covered a cattle gate. You know what a cattle gate is?"

I nodded. "Those parallel pipes on farm roads. Cars can drive across them, but animals can't walk across them."

"Ben said they got about a foot of snow down at the farm, wet, sticky snow. Covered the cattle gate, so Jake didn't see it and ran across it. His little feet went through, and his stomach got hung up on two of those pipes. He couldn't reach far enough forward to get a grip on the pipe in front of him, so he hung there, all four of his little fat legs running like hell and Jake going nowhere. Ben said Jake finally stopped struggling and looked him as if to say, 'A little help here?' Ben said he couldn't do anything, he was laughing so hard. So he went and plucked him off the cattle guard. Saved him again," Schappe recalled, looking down at the bar and laughing at the memory. "Ben could tell a story."

"That was the kind of girl Sue was," Tom said, putting a damper on the humor. "Couldn't stand to see an animal suffer. She just looked at that little dog at the vet's office and fell in love with him, that little beagle face and big velvet ears. When Sue fell in love, Sue fell seriously in love. Same with Ben. Not like my ex."

"You got an ex?"

"Yup. Two and a half years of wedded bliss. I should have read our wedding vows before the wedding. I think they said, 'Till death do us part, or two and half years, whichever comes first,'" Tom said, emptying his mug.

I ordered another beer for the three of us. I liked Schappe. Unlike a lot of bar owners, he'd sit there and drink with you, not say something like "I'm on duty" like he was a cop or something.

"Was this dog a hunter?" I asked.

"Sure was," Tom said. "But he'd only hunt for Sue, and Sue wasn't a hunter. Ben said the two of them would take walks, and Jake would run nearby and flush rabbit after rabbit. He said one time, Jake ran a rabbit right between the two of them. The rabbit ran by, and neither Sue nor Ben had a gun. Ben said Jake came puffing up over the hill and looked at them as if to say, 'Why didn't you shoot that damned rabbit?'"

"Ben said he took the dog out hunting once. He went in one direction, and Sue went in the other. Ben had Jake on a leash, 'cause he knew the dog, given a choice, would stick with Sue. He waited until he thought they were about five miles apart, and let Jake loose. Jake took off, but not to hunt. He went to go look for Sue. And found her, miles away, cross a couple hills, woods, creek. Amazing nose on that dog. Ben didn't see him again until Sue came in from her walk. That dog'd only hunt for her, his way of thanking her, I guess, for saving his life."

"So what happened to Jake?" I asked.

Schappe and Tom looked at one another, like some quiz show host had stumped the both of them. Finally Schappe said, "We think he's with Ben. He ain't around here. We all looked for him after Ben disappeared. We figured the cops wouldn't think of that angle. We kept checking at the pound, put ads in the paper, put posters up. That dog there," Schappe said pointing at the wall.

I could see why this particular beagle might stand out in a crowd of the breed. First of all, his face was almost white. Old dog, I thought. Second, he was fat. Most beagles, especially hunting dogs, are pretty lean. Looking at that picture of a fat dog with stubby little bow legs, I could visualize Jake being high-centered on a cattle guard. Third, Jake's back saddle was almost black, like a shepherd's, not light brown or tan like most beagles.

I noticed something else. Whoever took the picture was a good photographer. Jake's face filled the frame so you could see every detail, even his whiskers against a dark, blurred background. Whoever took the picture knew something about focus and depth of field. And Jake was smiling. Some dogs can smile, and Jake was clearly grinning. Happy dog, I thought.

"Who took the picture?"

"Sue did," Schappe said. "She was an excellent photographer."

"Sure was," I said. "I'm in the publishing business, and that would be a magazine quality shot. If that dog was around here, and you guys put posters up, someone would have found him."

"Oh yeah. We put posters all over the place. We raised $1,000 for a reward from the regulars and anyone else we could con into making a donation, plus Tom here raised about $300 on the pool table from unwilling donors. Ben was pretty well liked. We had this idea if we found the dog, we'd find a clue about what happened to Ben, and Ben's condo, for that matter," Schappe said.

"Ben's condo?"

Tom and Schappe traded that look again. Schappe shrugged. "Ben's condo disappeared not long after Ben disappeared," he said, giving me a Believe It Or Don't look.

I shrugged too. "I think I've been in enough bars to know when I'm being fed a story. There a punch line here? His house disappeared?"

"Honest. I knew where he lived - No. 11 at Lakeside Landing, right on Lake St. John. We all knew where he lived. We had some great parties there," Tom said. "Except you go to Lakeside Landing now, there are only 10 condos down by the lake. They've never heard of any Ben Clayton."

"This is getting a little weird," I said. "We've only had three beers."

"Four," Schappe said. "And number five coming. On me." He put his elbows on the bar and looked at me. "And that ain't all. Ben ran three McDonalds in this town. Now, almost six months after he's gone, only the McDonald's on Fifth Street remembers him. The other two say he never worked there. We know he managed those places. I say we, Tom and I and a couple other guys. It's damn peculiar, but a bunch of guys that used to come in here don't remember Ben all that well. Some who didn't come in here very often, don't remember him at all.

"Hell, he used to do what amounted to stand-up comedy in here. Guy tried to buy him a drink one time. 'No thanks,' Ben said. 'I got pretty drunk last night.' The guy says, 'How drunk?' Ben says, 'Let me put it this way. Me and Jerry were sitting at that table over there. One of us got up to take a piss, and the other guy sat there trying to figure out which one of us left.'"

Tom guffawed. "Yeah, and you didn't want to argue with him. He'd put you down quick. One night, he told this idiot, 'I'm not going to argue with a guy with a room temperature IQ.' Took the idiot a half hour to figure out he'd been insulted."

"I don't understand. You guys remember him, you remember Sue, and the dog. What're you trying to say, that the memories of these two are fading out, is that what you think?" I asked.

Tom and Schappe got serious again. Schappe said, "We think so. We don't remember as much about him as we think we should. I mean, we were all in the Jaycees for, I don't know, how long Tom?"

Tom started to say something, then shook he head. "I don't know. I joined in '89. I think Ben was a member when I joined, so I don't know when he joined."

"See, I don't think Ben was a member in '89. I don't think he joined until we got the softball team going in '92," Schappe said.

"He was the first coach, wasn't he?" said this guy behind me. He'd apparently wandered over to join the conversation. I turned around and offered a hand. "Al Schaffer," I said.

"Doug McInnis," he said, shaking my hand.

"Doug and Ben were pretty good friends, partners at that farm," Schappe explained.

"So what's your take on all this," I asked.

"Have another beer, and I'll give you my theory," Doug said.

"Have another beer and a shot, if you want Doug's theory," Tom said.

"And some drugs," Schappe said, turning to get more beer. "Why don't you guys just get a pitcher. It'd be cheaper, and I wouldn't have to make so many trips to the tap."

"Fine with me," I said. "I got girlfriend woes, job woes, IRS woes. Right now, I'm looking at the world through woes-colored glasses."

Doug chuckled. "You remind me a little bit of Ben. You read science fiction?"

"I read everything. I read books for a living. I'm a copy editor for McGregor Publishing over in Brookfield. I live here, work there."

"You ever read anything about alternate universes?" Doug asked.

"Here we go," Tom muttered.

"Hey, bald-on-top, you haven't come up with any other answer," Doug snapped.

"So true," Tom conceded.

"Ben used to tell me there's no purer love than a dog has for a good master. Or mistress, in this case. It's clear, unwavering, unquestioning. He'd say a dog doesn't care if its master is pretty or pretty ugly; black, white, green; drunk, sober; whatever. A dog's love is unequivocal; total, absolute," Doug remembered.

"You want an Absolut?" Schappe said, returning.

"No," Doug said. "I was talking about dogs," and him and Schappe got into it about something.

I don't have a dog. I'm never home, so it wouldn't be fair. I've got a girlfriend, though. Or had. We go together two years. She's almost living at my house. I go away for one week, and she jumps in bed with some guy who hangs out at our bar. Then lies to me about it, like I won't find out. Then she admits it, says she'll love me forever. Except now, she's going to live with a guy on a boat in Seattle. Maybe you wouldn't want your woman to be a dog, but that kind of love would be refreshing in humans.

"I'm sorry," I said. Doug had been saying something, and I'd been lost in my thoughts.

"I said Sue was killed driving back from the farm. There's a cliff along Highway 7, and a rock fell off the cliff. Big sucker, weighed about 650 pounds. Went right through her windshield, killed her instantly."

"You're kidding."

"True story. If she'd have driven by one second later, or one second earlier, she'd be sitting in that chair right now," Ed said, pointing to the still-empty stool. There must have been 30 people in the bar now. Schappe's wife had come in and was tending bar, plus they had a waitress and a cook on duty. I hadn't even noticed the place filling up. But no one was sitting in Sue's spot, right next to our little group.

"Where was Ben when that happened?"

"About a half hour behind her. He'd had to work late in town, so they'd taken two cars down to the farm. They were driving back, one after the other. He drove up on the accident scene right after it happened, police and fire trucks all over the place. He knew something bad had happened to Sue."

"I thought he was the first one on the scene," Tom said. "Didn't he call it in?"

"Naw, he didn't even have a cell phone then," Doug said, shaking his head.

"Yes he did. He just didn't have it in that old Chevy pickup he drove down to the farm," Schappe said.

"I thought that was Sue's pickup," Tom said.

"Whatever," Doug said in a tone that indicated it wasn't important. "The accident scene was along this cliff next to a big meadow. There's a stream that runs through that meadow, then some hills beyond."

"What's that got to do with anything?" I asked.

"Cause that's where Ben went the day he disappeared. He took Jake with him, drove down there, and nobody's seen hide nor hair of the man or the dog since. You know why?"

"Why?" I asked.

"Cause him and that dog found Sue," he said, slapping his hand on the bar. "More beer," he shouted in no particular direction. Schappe just grimaced. His wife grinned and started filling another pitcher. Must have been some bar ritual, I thought.

"Bullcrapo," Tom said, pulling out some money to pay for this round. "He went looking for Sue, right enough, but him and that dog fell down some sinkhole in the woods. That's why they've never been found."

"So what happened to his truck?" Schappe said, taking the pitcher from his wife.

"It's probably sitting in the front yard of some Ozark trailer home right now, right next to a couch and a fat kid with dirt around his mouth. You've seen some of those guys down there - eyes really, really close together," Tom said. "You know what a family tree looks like in the Ozarks?"

"What?"

"No branches."

"Talk about old jokes," I said. "So Doug, didn't he have any family or anything? What did the police down there say."

Doug laughed. "No family, and let's just say the sheriff down there isn't an FBI Academy graduate. I don't think they've solved a felony down there in ten years. They spend most of their time trying to catch floaters on the river smoking dope. Last time I checked, the sheriff couldn't even remember the case."

"So you think he's in another dimension?" I asked.

"You've read about this. You know how it works. Every time we make a decision, we create another dimension. There's one where I decided to come here today, and one where I didn't; two different time lines."

"And there's one where I think you're an idiot, and one where I actually pay attention to you," Tom said.

"Shut up, Tom. Let 'im finish," Schappe said.

"I'm familiar with that. It's one of the oldest plot lines in science fiction. They write whole books, hell, whole series of books based on alternate time lines, alternative histories, like if Germany had won World War II," I said.

"Right, like that. So Ben says, 'Suppose Sue had left the house five seconds later. Two seconds. She's going 60 mph down the highway, a mile a minute. That's 88 feet per second. She leaves one second earlier, a half second earlier, that rock misses her by 40 feet. Her dimension could be that close,' he said, holding his thumb and index finger so close they were almost touching. 'But the longer I wait, the further it goes away. I've got to go now,' Ben said."

"I asked him, how are you going to find this dimension? He said, 'I'm not. Jake will. He could always find Sue, no matter where she was. And he wants to, I can tell. He looks at me like he's saying 'Gimme a chance, Ben, please.' So I gotta go. It's been real. I love you guys, I really do. But this is Sue.' And that was the last I ever saw of him," Doug concluded.

"That's the last anyone ever saw of him," Schappe added.

I thought about that for a moment. "Then why the chair, if they're both gone?" I asked.

Schappe kind of dithered for a moment, then said something he probably wouldn't have said if he hadn't been drinking. "We want 'em back here. I thought maybe if there was some kind of anchor to draw them back, if they're that close…"

After that, the conversation kind of veered away from Ben, Sue and Jake and got lost in a haze of beer, pool games, life stories and "Hey, man, you're the best" kind of backslapping and professions of love and friendship you only hear when everybody's drunk and doesn't have to prove out the next day.

I staggered out of there about midnight because I couldn't speak anymore. At least, I couldn't speak English. I do remember, though, as I stumbled out the door, that Sue's chair was empty. There must have been 60 people jammed into that little bar, but no one sat on Sue's stool.

I spent the next day on the couch nursing my hangover and thinking about life and love. I really liked Tammi, but did I love her? Would I do anything for her, like Jake would do for Sue? Or like Ben did? Would I drop everything and go traipsing across some tick-infested meadow and into the Ozarks on the very long chance that some dumb dog could find her? Probably not.

I think I liked the sex, and she was a beauty. I don't know what she saw in a potato face like me, but it was fun having her around, showing her off. Then again, it wasn't like Ben and Sue. What'd he do, I wondered. Just let Jake out and start across that field, into the woods? Jeez, Ben could have spent the next few days following Jake, who was probably following a rabbit, who was probably wondering why he got picked on by a couple nut cases that day, one a delusional dog with an excellent nose, and one a sad and confused man.

I figured Tom was probably right. Jake probably fell in a sinkhole, and Ben, being Ben, went in after him. The Ozarks are full of holes and caves like that. The two of them probably starved to death in a wet, cold, dark pit nobody's ever marked on a topo map. But what a great story, I thought, even if it wasn't true. Ben's friends had told me Ben and Sue hadn't hit it off right away, but Sue got dumped by her boyfriend. Ben had been hanging around in case something like that happened. He'd loved her from the moment he'd seen her. And she'd found in him what she'd been looking for over 15 years and a dozen guys.

Wouldn't that whole story be wonderful if it was true, I thought. What if Ben and Jake followed Sue over just a little bit into another dimension where that rock missed her car by 40 feet. It was like he said. It wasn't a big change, like Germany winning the war. It was just a little change, a slight deviation located not too far away from here.

I read dog books too. This one writer was trying to make a case that dogs have more than five senses, although those five senses are pretty good. But how does a dog in the back of one car with the windows rolled up going 50 mph down a road know there's dog in the back of another car going 50 mph in the opposite direction? They do. They get up, start barking. That other car goes by in the opposite direction, and you see a dog there barking at your dog. How do they do that?

Jake could find Sue anytime, anywhere, Doug had said. Even in a nearby dimension? Maybe so. That's strong love, I thought, the kind I'd like to find. I could see Jake, the fat little dog with stubby legs, taking a whiff of the air, then taking off, certain he was going in the right direction, to Sue. It wouldn't have mattered to Jake if Ben was following or not. In the little dog's mind, this would be complete dedication to his mistress. He would be on a mission to find her if for no other reason than she might need him for something. And if she didn't need him, he'd lie down near her and wait, like Ben had waited for Sue.

And the reason that people were forgetting about Ben? That records and physical evidence about his existence in this dimension were disappearing? That's easy; there has to be a balance. If some irresistible force, like the unbending determination of a dog to find his mistress, skews the balance between dimensions, more malleable forces will shift the correct that imbalance. All the forces in the universe couldn't deter Jake, so other realities had to change.

Wasn't that an interesting thought; the love of a little beagle up against the forces of the universe. People still remembered Sue. She died in her own time and place. But Ben and Jake? They were over there when they should be here. The universe was correcting that little anomaly. It would be like a stretched rubber band snapping back to its original linear shape.

So that was really the answer, I thought. If we do forget entirely about Ben and Jake, if there is no record of them ever being here, then Ben didn't just die in some sinkhole; he made it. Jake led him across the meadow, through those woods, up into the hills and across whatever kind of line separated the dimensions to find Sue. What a trip, I thought. What a love.

Then the phone rang and interrupted my musings. It was Tammi.

"Al, can I come over. I really need to talk to you. It's good news, I promise. I just need to see you," she said.

"I don't think so, Tammi. I think we're history. I'm looking for something a little more permanent that what you've got in mind."

"Al, I love you. That's what I wanted to tell you. Please let me come over. We can talk about it."

You wouldn't know love if it walked up and poked you in the eye, I thought, but didn't say it. "Tammi, I learned something about myself yesterday. You can have any guy you want, Jim in Seattle or Mike down at the bar. Not me. We're not going to work out. You'd hang around a while, but you'd end up dumping me for some young, handsome buck. I learned a little bit about true love yesterday. I want one girl, one wife, someone who will stay with me till I die," I said.

Or even after I die, I thought. There was more conversation, but it was meaningless.

I started going to Schappe's place pretty regularly, until I got sent out of town for computer training at the company's headquarters. It took six weeks. Then I had a couple more weeks of sharing my new knowledge with several trainees at the plant in Brookfield. That kept me pretty busy.

It was three months before I got back to Schappe's. It was a Friday night, and the place was real busy. He had a band that night, a local group that was popular in town. I had to kind of walk sideways just to get in, and of course, every seat at the bar was taken.

I felt vaguely disturbed about there not being an empty seat at the bar, even with that big crowd, but I couldn't figure out why something like that would bother me.

The Winter of Bauer's Discontent

It had been another nasty scene at work. Mike was steaming as he drove home through the heavy evening traffic, and he was still steaming at dinner two hours later.

"You know what I should have said? I should have said this whole company is run like a Dilbert cartoon," Mike said.

"Why didn't you say that? Knowing you, you probably thought of it," said Kay, his significant other. Or sort of his significant other. "What was it this time?"

"Remember last week when the sewer collapsed?"

"Of course, I remember. You worked all day and practically all night on it. Saved us about $800."

At least that amount, Mike thought. He owned a house that was about 90 years old. Under most of the house, there was only a crawl space. The cast iron sewer pipe had become so thin that, when Mike dug it up, he could poke a screwdriver through it. Dirt from the crawl space had started falling in the sewer pipe, which plugged it and backed up the toilets.

First, Mike had to dig from the outside. He had the sense to dig a big enough hole so when the accumulated sewage from a two-story house came spewing out, it didn't run all over the lawn. Then he had to dig up the ruined pipe while hunched over in the crawl space. That was no fun. Then he had to mate the new plastic pipe with the old cast-iron pipe section that was still good.

He'd come out of the crawl space dirty and smelly - particularly smelly - and hacking up the fine dirt that hung in the air down there. He sported numerous bumps from banging his head against the beams supporting the floor and abrasions from dealing with old cast iron pipe, and he probably should get a tetanus shot.

But all in all, he felt pretty good about doing the job himself. If the plumber had done it, the bill would have been about $1,400. With the work Mike did, it only cost about $600, and part of that was the unavoidable inspection.

Course, he had to take a day off work. But he had 151 sick days accumulated, and every employee had 3 personal days each year. He didn't think that would be a problem until he got to work the following day.

Arnie called him in to the office. "I see you took an emergency day yesterday," Arnie said.

"Yeah. My sewer collapsed. It took a day to fix it."

"Just for the record, I'm sympathetic when employees need to take emergency leave," Arnie said, speaking as if the employees were his personal servants. "Next time, however, I'll require more notice before you take an emergency leave."

Mike just stared at him for several moments. "Um, I didn't plan for this to happen, Arnie."

"Of course you didn't. But sewers just don't collapse. They wear out. You should have seen this coming and scheduled the work for one of your regular days off. Then we don't have your personal problems disrupting the whole work schedule," Arnie said, as if talking to a 10-year-old.

Mike started to answer that, but Arnie held up his hand as if to stop traffic. "I'm not going to get into a big argument about this. I'm just telling you to be a little more considerate of your co-workers next time. You know we had to call someone in to take your place," Arnie said.

Mike wanted to say, Of course, you had to call someone in. You've called me in plenty of times to replace someone else. Or he wanted to say, Why didn't you jump in and do my job for one day? Because you don't know how, you big lump. Or, That isn't part of the contract, that we have to give notice for emergency days. That's why they're called 'emergency' days. What if I'd cut my arm off with a chain saw? Would you require more notice for that?

But he didn't say any of those things. He just walked out of the office fuming, got out of work as soon as he could and drove home, vowing to take a sick day tomorrow just for revenge. But he didn't do that either.

Maybe I should just go home and beat the dog, he thought, but then realized he didn't have a dog anymore. About three months ago, Mike had put Zeke to sleep, Zeke, his companion of 12 years. What a great dog, Mike thought. I miss him a lot.

That depressed him even more. Mike wasn't having a good year. The job wasn't going well. He'd had some offers to go elsewhere, but he couldn't seem to pull the trigger on that decision. Changing jobs probably would mean moving to another town, a big undertaking. The move would have advanced his career, but staying was easier. And that was the way Mike was making most of his decisions lately - whatever was easier.

He would have liked to talk to Kay about the problem, but Kay was kind of an airhead. She was a woman who spent from 30 minutes to an hour every morning putting on makeup. Besides, she was out with George tonight. She didn't exactly tell him that, but she wasn't a very good liar.

"Would you like to go down to The Pub after I get off work tonight?" he'd asked.

"Um, no I can't. My daughter's supposed to call tonight, you know, the one with the husband," she'd said, saying the word "husband" like one would say the word “wart.” Mike should have responded with, “Well, why don’t you just take the call on your cell phone? She would have come up with something even more lame than the original excuse. “Oh, you can’t talk in a bar,” for instance. His next move would have been, “Well, why don’t we just stay home, and you can take the call here,” until he’d had her checkmated, at which point he should have said, “Why don’t you just damn well admit you’re going out with George!”

But he didn’t do that either. So Mike didn’t have her to talk to, nor did he have Zeke to talk to. Dogs never lie, he thought. They don’t dump you for other humans just because the other humans are younger, or better looking, or richer. He had a sneaking suspicion Kay was trying to figure out which one of them, him or George was richer before she made any decision. I am not going to help here with that, he thought. I am gonna get another dog, he mentally added.

On Mike’s next day off, he called his friend John Morgan to see if he knew of any dogs currently available. Morgan was a veterinarian, and Mike figured John would not pawn off some problem dog on him.

“Got one right here,” Morgan said.

The dog’s name was Roscoe. Morgan identified Roscoe’s ancestry vaguely as some sort of Australian shepherd. Its fur was mottled brown and black, sort of like camouflage, and the fur was coarse. Long, heavy whiskers hung from around his mouth like the mustachios of a Mexican bandit. He had big, brown eyes that seemed to say, “Trust me.”

Mike was a little hesitant. He asked Morgan why a full-grown shepherd that seemed so friendly was up for adoption. “His former owners have that cabinet shop up on 94. They were trying to train him as a sentry dog. It didn’t work out. I guess he wasn’t mean enough,” Morgan said.

That’s a plus, Mike thought. I don’t want a vicious dog.

"They weren't too subtle about their training methods, if you know what I mean," Morgan said. "This guy needs a good home."

Dog and man looked at one another. The man was thinking, This would probably be a pretty good dog. The dog was thinking...actually, who the hell knows what a dog is thinking? All we know is Roscoe walked over to Mike, leaned against the man and flashed his best doggy smile, a smile that Mike thought had a little mischief behind it.

So Mike took him home to a small, tidy house in town on maybe a 5,000-square-foot lot. Not a big yard by any measure, but the six-foot stockade fence that surrounded the back yard lent it the feeling of privacy in a neighborhood where the houses were scarcely 50 feet apart.

The fence actually was built for Mike's previous dog, Zeke, who could leap six-feet straight up from a standing start. "An NBA prospect," a friend had observed.

"National Basketball Association?"

"No Brains Apparent," the friend said, watching Zeke bounce up and down, trying to grab a stick in Mike's upraised hand.

Roscoe didn't look nearly as athletic as Zeke. Roscoe next to Zeke was Charlie Chaplin's Little Hobo next to Cary Grant's Rhett Butler. Where Zeke strode, Roscoe shambled; where Zeke was alert, Roscoe was indolent. Zeke resembled Steve McQueen in "The Great Escape;" Roscoe resembled Schultz in "Hogan's Heroes."

So Mike introduced Roscoe to the backyard - Stalag 2859 Elm - without a thought that the dog could escape.

What Roscoe saw was a basic, fenced backyard. The house sat on the west end of the yard. A detached garage formed a square intrusion into the southeast corner of the yard. The fence ran from the east end of the garage to the northeast corner of the yard, then east to connect with the house. Another fence ran from the south side of the house to a corner, then east to connect with the garage. Full enclosure. Roscoe took in the layout like an experienced con.

The dog jumped off the steps leading to the back door of the house and scouted the fence. There was one gate in the west fence. He pushed his head against the gate and discovered it was latched.

"You trying to get out, fella?" Mike asked. "This yard is a lot like life. You're dumped into it, you look around, you're interested for a while. Then you realize that's all you got, and it ain't much. Then you spend the rest of your life lying on the stairs, waiting for someone to tell you what to do."

"Mike! C'mon! We're going to be late," Kay shouted from inside the house.

"See, Roscoe?" Mike said to the dog, who had returned from his scout to lean against Mike's leg. "I'm coming," Mike shouted back at the house.

After Mike went inside, Roscoe began a more thorough examination of his yard. The fence, he understood. The garage had an opening for a door, but no door, He went in. The garage had a cool, cement floor beneath several tables. He smelled the wood and shavings and tools that he had smelled at his last home, and whimpered a little. He hadn't liked his last home. He noticed openings in the walls, too. Apparently, Mike hadn't gotten around to installing windows in the garage.

At the back of the garage were two swinging doors. Roscoe pushed on them. The doors yielded a little, but a chain on the outside prevented them from opening. The dog looked at the doors as if weighing their vulnerability, then went back outside. He followed the fence around the yard, stopping from time to time to mark territory he now considered his. A small garden interrupted his traverse of the yard. The dog sniffed in disdain, and peed on that too.

On the other side of the fence along the north side of the yard, Roscoe detected the odor of a human child. Children were good. "Oh, Mr. Mike's got a new dog," the child exclaimed. "Can you come play wif me? What a good dog," Leslie cooed.

Roscoe wagged his tail furiously. Children were good, and usually meant food. At that moment, Mike stuck his head out the door. "Leslie, don't tease him. He's a new dog."

"Mr. Mike, can I play wif him?"

"No, Leslie, I don't know too much about him, and he's too big for you anyway. I'll bring him over to meet you tomorrow. I've gotta go now. Bye."

"Aw, he never let me play wif Zekey either," the little girl said through the fence. "You want to play wif me, don't you?" she said, addressing the dog.

Mike returned home about four hours later to find Roscoe lying on the front porch. That would be the front porch on the west side of the house, the porch overlooking the front yard, the porch that was not within the confines of the fence.

I must have left the gate unlatched, Mike thought, leading Roscoe back to the Stalag. Mike closed the gate firmly, checked the latch, and went to bed. Or almost went to bed. "Michael, I can't go out Friday night. I promised George I'd go shopping with him. I told him before, but I'd forgotten. I'm sorry. You don't mind, do you?" Kay said breezily.

Do I mind? Of course I mind, Mike thought. Am I going to say anything? If I say what I think, will I ruin my chances with her for good?

"I've already got tickets, Kay. Can't you go shopping with George on Saturday?"

"Um, no," Kay said. Kay always prefaced her lies with "um." The "um" was kind of drawn out as she looked at a far wall, or the ceiling. It gave her time to think of something. "We're taking his niece with us to get a present, and I need to go along. Call me next week," Kay said as she hurried out the door.

Why do I put up with this? Mike thought. Cause you love her, stupid. She isn't worth it, Mike thought. So walk away, stupid, call up Robbie. She wants to go out with you. But starting over on a whole new relationship was for Mike like starting a new job; too much effort.

It was a warm September night in Missouri. Roscoe thought about going out too, but ended up going into the garage, resting his head on the cool concrete and going to sleep. The dog awoke about 4 a.m. and went outside to sample the plethora of smells offered up by the neighborhood, including the odor of a friendly female of the species.

Roscoe went to the gate, shoved his nose between the gate and the gate post, and pushed hard. There was enough play in the bottom of the gate that a moderately strong dog could shove its way through; Roscoe was more than moderately strong. He went through easily. Behind him, the gate snapped shut again, leaving no evidence of his method of egress.

Mike found him asleep on the front porch in the morning.

"Roscoe! This has got to stop, buddy. We've got leash laws in this city," Mike said, looking furtively at the house to the south, home of the Gulates. Roscoe didn't know what a leash law was, and didn't care. He nuzzled up against Mike, and looked up at him with love in those bandit eyes. The dog obediently followed Mike around the south side of the house and back into the yard.

Mike went back to the front porch, thought a moment, then yelled, "Roscoe, Roscoe! Come, boy. C'mon Roscoe," he called, then ran inside to look out the bay window on the south side of the house just in time to see the dog push his way through the gate.

He ran back outside and grabbed the dog. He gave him a good scratch and a "good dog" for coming when called, and led him back to the back yard. *I didn't do such a good job on that gate*, he thought. *Kay mentioned that. I can do better.* So he chained Roscoe in the back yard, went to the hardware store, and returned with the materials to do the job right.

It took all afternoon, but when he was done, Mike felt a little pride in his workmanship. The gate now dovetailed nicely with the end posts of the fence - solid, secure. A little pride was a feeling he had felt very little of recently.

Roscoe had different feelings about the work. Not that the dog had a clue about what Mike was doing. He'd find out in his own good time that the escape route through the gate had been eliminated. What he also had found out was that if he came when Mike called, he might end up on a chain all afternoon. A few moments of ear-scratch and "good dog" were mostly eclipsed by a long afternoon on the chain.

Mike had a late shift that day, and made it to work almost in time. "Nice to see you coming in on time for once, on time for you being within 15 minutes of when you're supposed to be here," Arnie commented.

"Sorry, I'm sorry, I've been having some domestic problems at home. I think they're taken care of," Mike said.

"That would be understandable if you were married. You're not married," Arnie observed.

"Well, I've got this new dog that keeps getting out. With my neighbors, it's a real problem," Mike explained.

"So I guess 'cause you've got a problem with your dog, you're entitled to work shorter hours than everyone else in the department?"

"I didn't say that. I'll stay later to make up for it."

"I know you will," Arnie said, and turned and left.

Joe Jerkins came over to Mike's desk. "If I were you, and Arnie was Arnie, I'd tell him if he was unhappy with my work, find someone else to do it. He can't do your job. No one here can do your job as well as you do. You work harder than anyone else in this shop, and he jumps on you for being a little late."

"Where am I going to get another job that pays $1,000 a week, Joe."

"You're union. The only union employee this company's fired in the last decade was Sheila Hendrikson, and she asked to be fired. They'd just transfer you. What else can they do, make you work nights and weekends?" Joe said.

That was an old joke in this department. Mike and everybody else in the photo department already worked nights and weekends. "Well, I was late. If I wasn't late, I guess I would have argued with him," Mike said. "I'd better get to this."

After Mike left for work, Roscoe wandered over to the fence. The kids had gotten home from school, and little Leslie was playing in her back yard just north of Mike's back yard. Roscoe was lonely; he wanted to play with Leslie. He'd found out that the gate wasn't available any more, so he nuzzled the low latch on the garden gate open and started digging in the soft dirt of the garden. In 15 minutes, he was under the fence and playing with Leslie and her friends, and glarming some free treats.

When Leslie's mother called her in for dinner, Roscoe went and met some other dogs from nearby neighborhoods. They wandered around like a small teenage gang until about midnight, when he went home. Having made the connection between being caught outside the yard and being chained, he returned to the backyard by way of the tunnel.

Because Leslie's mother told him, Mike knew Roscoe was getting out, but he didn't know how. He inspected the back yard but didn't think to look in the garden because the garden was surrounded by a four-foot tall fence. He didn't find the tunnel until he actually did some gardening a week or so later. The days were getting colder, and it was time to dig up and turn the garden.

"I'll fix this, he thought, and drove down to the river to get some of the most jagged rocks he could find. He put the rocks in Roscoe's tunnel, along with some scrap boards with nails driven through them. "You put your feet in here, or try to crawl through, it's going to hurt, Roscoe. I'm just warning you," Mike told his dog.

Roscoe looked at his source of food (most of the time) and tried to look contrite. Mike bent down and hugged his dog. "Aw. it's okay, big dog. I just can't have you running around the block like you do. Most of the neighbors understand, but the Gulates will call the dogcatcher. You'll have to spend the night in jail, and I'll have to pay a fine."

And he really hated the thought of giving his unpleasant neighbors that kind of satisfaction. He still was mad about Anne mowing down all his day lilies along the border between their two lots. "Sorry, Mike, but the goddamn lilies were spreading into my garden," she'd said.

"Anne, you can't come over and mow my flowers just because you don't like 'em. How'd you like it if I did that to your garden?"

"You'd better not," she'd said, and sauntered away.

What I ought to do is go get my lawn mower, mow those flowers, and see what happens. Don isn't tough enough to do anything, Mike thought, but as usual, ended up doing nothing. "The day lilies will grow back," he'd told Kay.

"And Brenda will mow them again."

"I'll think of something, so she won't," Mike said, but couldn't think of anything offhand that would prevent the whole embarrassing incident from occurring again. After shutting off Roscoe's tunnel, Mike looked darkly at his neighbor's house to the south. They let their dog out at night, he knew. They owned a fancy purebred German shorthair, but they didn't want its fancy, purebred German shorthair dog shit in their yard, so the dog got to run at night. Then they turned in other people whose dogs got out. Lousy hypocrites, Mike thought.

"You stay in the yard, okay?" Mike told his dog, as if dogs understood English. Roscoe wagged his tail. He recognized "yard" and "stay." The dog figured he'd better stay in the yard for a couple nights anyway, just till the heat was off. That resolution lasted until he smelled that smell no normal, red blooded (and unneutered) dog could resist.

Without hesitation, he went to the tunnel and carefully lifted out all the nailed boards and rocks with his mouth. Mike had thoughtfully picked jagged rocks that Roscoe could get a grip on. Smooth rocks would have been tougher, but with these, Roscoe was out of the yard and on his way to his date in 10 minutes flat. He'd always had a yen for a German shorthair.

Fortunately for Mike, the Gulates weren't the smartest people in the world. In fact, they were pretty far down on the list of people whose opinions might interest anyone. They didn't know who had knocked up their AKC registered pet; they couldn't tell from the coloring of the pups who the hell the father was. Roscoe's coloring and that of a German shorthair were pretty close. The pups were pretty smart, and they all had long, Mexican mustachios, but that didn't seem to please the Gulates. They called city Animal Control.

Mike was right in that the Gulates didn't like to handle things themselves. Their kid was a rowdy and a thief who couldn't get through an entire sentence without using the F-word, but the Gulates railed against other people's kids in particular and juvenile delinquents in general. Nobody else's yard was good enough, and those unkempt yards lowered everyone's property values, they'd tell anyone who would listen. They told other people to park their old cars in the alleys while Don worked on his car in the front yard. And they got along well with the Animal Control people, who had a collective IQ right up there with Anne's.

She ratted on Mike, so the Animal Control folks, with no more evidence than her allegation, trooped over to Mike's house, Anne following behind. "You're welcome to look. I'm sure you'll agree, there's no way my dog could get out of the yard," Mike said, wishing that was true. Of course if you broke down that sentence, he hadn't exactly lied. "There's no way my dog could get out of the yard" was a blatant lie. The "I'm sure you'll agree" coupled with the sentence made it not a lie. Mike was sure they'd agree.

While the Animal Control people and Anne were blathering, Mike thought about the cause of his current problem - Roscoe. The dog knew Mike got mad when he left the yard, the dog knew that. He went anyway. Roscoe was his own dog. If Mike couldn't handle that, why, Roscoe would go find another human, like he'd done before. So why was Mike standing there putting up with this nonsense. You're always afraid you're going to permanently offend someone. Do you want these people as your friends? "Anne, what are you doing here?" he asked. Before she could answer, he added, "Go back to your own house. I'm sure you know you're not welcome here."

"I'm with them. I'm the injured party," she said. Mike got in front of the whole group, eyeballing the lead animal control lady. "Now's the time when you show me where it's your job to establish paternity for people's dogs. Show me the ordinance. And show me the ordinance where you can allow non-officers to trespass on my property."

"It's our job to enforce animal control ordinances, Mr. Bauer."

"So what ordinance did I violate?"

Lady animal control fidgeted and looked at her companions and hesitated, so Mike, having already taken the plunge, bored on. "The only reason you're here is because Anne here called you and made some accusation. That's all you know. What is it, do you work for her? This city's got a population of 50,000, and there are three of you here in my yard on a paternity case. Would you like me to call the newspaper about this?"

That did it for lady animal control. "Mr. Bauer, I'd better not catch your dog running without a leash, and I'm going to be looking. Mrs. Gulate, we really can't do anything about your dog. That's something you'll have to pursue as a civil matter."

"And I will," Anne said.

"Go ahead. Spend your money," Mike said.

He told Kay about the incident later, and she looked at him with a quizzical look in her eye. "I thought you weren't any good at confrontations," she said.

"I got fed up," Mike said, but thought, it's the dog. He's teaching me new tricks.

After that, Mike stormed into the back yard to glare at Roscoe. The dog flashed his "trust me" smile, which looked a little insincere, sandwiched as it was between those drooping mustachios. Mike stormed back out of the yard, and returned about an hour later with 100 feet of chicken wire and 14 bags of sackcrete.

Roscoe watched as his grim and determined master sweated and strained, digging a trench along the bottom of the fence. He then stapled chicken wire to the bottom of the fence, letting it hang down into the trench. Then he mixed up the cement and poured it into the trench. The following day when the cement had set, he filled the trench up with dirt.

"What I've done here," Mike explained to the dog, "is build an underground fence. Even if you dig a foot down, you're going to run into chicken wire. And you can't pull the chicken wire out like you pulled those rocks out of the tunnel, because it's anchored in concrete. This may be a game to you, but it's a game the most intelligent animal is going to win, and that's me."

Then Mike, sweaty and dirty and tired, stalked off into the house. Roscoe was polite enough to wait until about 3 a.m. before he walked to the back of the garage, pushed between the two big swinging doors, dug a little trench in the gravel driveway until it was deep enough to squeeze through the gap between the doors, and ran off into the night.

When Mike got up the next day, Roscoe was still out. He went looking for the errant dog. After walking around the block, he spotted Roscoe about two blocks away at the end of the alley. Roscoe spotted Mike about the same time Mike spotted Roscoe. "Roscoe! Come! Roscoe," Mike yelled.

Roscoe gauged the distance between them. All dogs have obedience zones. The greater the distance between dog and master, the greater the ability to disobey. It was an exact, proportional equation. Some dogs had totally given up their right to disobedience, shorn of their natural heritage by such developments as shock collars or short legs. Roscoe was not one of these dogs. He figured two blocks was about the MOD - maximum obedience distance - and took off.

Unfortunately, with his attention focused on Mike, he ran right into the noose of the dogcatcher who had been staking out Mike's neighborhood.

Mike witnessed what he wryly referred to as "the collar," but also realized that he was late again for work, and so couldn't bail Roscoe out until the next day. So Roscoe spent most of the night in doggy jail in a cage that had a cement floor (no digging his way out), chain link walls and ceiling (no chewing his way out) and about 30 other dogs jailed around him. Roscoe didn't like it there, and especially didn't like the big malamute in the cage next to him. The malamute didn't like him equally as well; Roscoe could sense that rather clearly.

It took Roscoe about two hours of worrying the gravity latch on the cage before the latch popped open, and the dog was into the run between two rows of cages. That got him out of his cell, but not out of prison. The run between the cages ended in a wall at one end and a closed door at the other end. So Roscoe got on top of the cages by climbing up a pile of dog food bags at the wall end of the run, and walked to the door end of the run across the tops of the cages, pausing only to pee on the malamute.

He got into the offices beyond the dog run by squeezing through a hole where a vent had been removed in preparation for painting the next day. Once in the offices, Roscoe walked around on the desks probing for a weak window. After a lot of pushing and lunging, he found one that would swing open much like the gate at Mike's house. Push came to shove, and he was gone!

Bob Branson, the chief animal control officer, arrived at his office the next day to find a window open and partially broken, papers and trash everywhere and all the dogs howling. This has burglary written all over it, he thought. This could be my chance to make it on to the police force.

Bob fancied himself somewhat more heroic than an animal control officer needed to be. Taking a gun from his vehicle - a gun that he was not supposed to have - he sidled in his best cop show imitation over to the front door. He ignored the thought that any self-respecting burglar would be long gone with the coming of the day.

Bob kicked open the front door (it being the city's door, not his) and rushed into the office area. There wasn't anyone there, but the whole place was in disarray. Pens, pencils, phones, blotters, calendars, fans, lights and other desktop paraphernalia were spread all over the place. It looked like clear evidence of a burglary until Bob got to looking closer and found no drawers opened, no filing cabinets ajar, nothing missing.

Then he found unmistakable evidence of what had actually occurred. What had once been dog food was deposited in bulk right in the middle of his desktop. Bob stared at that for a while, wondering why a dog would break into his office and poop on his desk. He knew the dogs in the town hated him, but this...Then in a rare flash of insight, Bob deduced that the culprit canine probably had left the building through the window, not entered.

But which dog? All the dogs in the kennels were checked in and where they were supposed to be. Bob started apprehending employees as they arrived, making them stand in front of his desk and be interrogated.

Kenneth O'Connell was the dogcatcher who nailed Roscoe the night before. This was just a part-time job for him while he attended the local college. O'Connell had had a date the night before, and hadn't had time to check Roscoe in. He figured he'd do it in the morning. As soon as he realized Ranger Bob, as the employees called him, didn't know who had shirked their duty the night before, O'Connell decided he wasn't going to help him out. "Don't know, Mr. Branson. Everything was shipshape and tidy when I left."

"And what time was that?" Bob asked.

"5 p.m., sharp, sir. The premises were secure, sir."

Bob suspected O'Connell was making fun of his penchant for running his department like a military unit, but the kid never seemed to cross the line into clear insubordination. Bob didn't fare any better with any of the other employees, not that they particularly wanted to help. Mainly, they wanted to get out of the office and laugh at the fact that Bob had been yanked by a dog. Bob had never, and would never discover the difference between being a boss and being a jerk.

One employee, however, saw an opportunity to settle a score over on Elm Street. "Mr. Branson, I don't know, but I bet one of the staff brought in that dog that's been the subject of complaints from the Gulates," she said. "The dog's an escape artist, runs every night."

"Why wouldn't they tell me that?" Bob asked.

"Because you'd fire them, sir." Cyndi (her parents had named her Cindy, but she hadn't thought that distinctive enough) wasn't afraid of Ranger Bob. She manipulated him regularly. Now she was using him to settle with that Mike Bauer, who had spoken so rudely to her. Unwittingly, she had targeted the right dog.

Ranger Bob was willing to pick on the wrong suspect if it was easier than finding the right one. "All right. We're going to put a watch on that neighborhood, and the next time that dog gets out, we'll have him for lunch," he decided.

"Um, that's going to involve some overtime, sir. The neighbors say the dog only gets out at night," Cyndi said, figuring she might as well make some money on this deal. Fat, slovenly and ill-mannered, she didn't have a social life that would be disrupted by night duty. As for the other employees, screw them.

Such is bureaucratic service. People worked there because they couldn't get or hold jobs in the real world, because the efficient administrators in other departments wanted them out of the way, or because they needed the money to go to school so they wouldn't have to do this work again for the rest of their lives.

"And sir, shouldn't you clean that dog shit off your desk?" Cyndi added. "It stinks in here."

After ordering someone to take care of that, Bob spent the rest of the day planning the operation. The more he thought about it, the more he developed a dislike for Roscoe. And when Ranger Bob disliked a dog, bad things happened to the animal. They usually went to the gas chamber a little earlier than the five days required under the ordinance.

"Oh, I'm sorry, Mr. Bauer," Bob rehearsed. "We had to put your dog to sleep under the vicious dog section of the city code. So sorry, but it's your fault, you know. It's your responsibility to keep your dog confined or on a leash. Just be glad we don't cite you personally for harboring a vicious animal, which we could." Yep, Bob thought, victory would be his.

Bob put three assistant junior dogcatchers plus himself on duty the following night, 60 percent of his staff. "I won't ask you people to do something I'm not willing to do myself," Bob said. O'Connell could hardly keep from laughing out loud.

The city had two animal control trucks, and Bob added his to the fleet. Bob's truck was a four-wheel drive pickup painted camouflage. All three trucks went up to the Elm Street neighborhood, and it wasn't long before they spotted Roscoe running with his gang through the night.

Bob drove down the alley to keep Roscoe in sight. He radioed Cyndi to cut off the other end of the alley. “O’Connell, I want you out on the left flank.”

“Yes sir, sir. Oh sir, which way are you going?”

Bob drew a blank on that one until he realized the answer to the question would determine which flank was on the left. “Fifth Street, you idiot,” he radioed.

“Yes sir. Over and out on Fifth Street.”

While Bob was wondering if he ought to fire O’Connell, he almost ran head-on into Cyndi coming from the south end of the alley. “Where’d he go,” Bob radioed, although Cyndi’s vehicle was only 15 feet away.

“I think he ran toward Randolph.”

“That’s behind me. I would have seen him go by.”

“It’s dark, sir,” O’Connell cut in. “It’s a brown and black dog. He could have blew by you,” he said, almost on key with Linda Ronstadt.

“He couldn’t have gotten by me. There are fences on either side of the alley,” Bob replied. “Ralph,” he called to the third dogcatcher, who was on foot. “See anything?”

Ralph was a fat old cuss who had got tired of reading meters for the city. Too much walking. He was just serving time until his pension kicked in. Ralph was sitting on his butt at the corner of Elm and Tecumseh, and hadn’t seen a thing. “Haven’t seen a thing, Bob” The mayor was Ralph’s cousin; he didn’t have to call Bob “sir.”

“There he is,” said Cyndi. “He’s running along Fifth Street.”

“I’m on his tail,” O’Connell radioed. Kenneth actually did drive down the street after Roscoe, but Roscoe had spent one night in doggy jail, and didn’t plan on spending another there. The dog recognized O’Connell’s truck, and made the connection with the other pursuers. It was like being chased by a pack; you didn't want to let them run you into exhaustion. So Roscoe sat until one of them got close, then bolted. Four people out in the open can't catch a dog that doesn't want to be caught, unless they shoot the dog. Bob wasn't quite stupid enough to do that in a residential neighborhood.

Bob drove down Randolph toward Fifth Street, and saw Roscoe run into the alley. Cyndi was at the other end, the north end this time. "We've got him, Cyndi. Drive toward the fences." They met in the middle of the alley. "Where'd he go?" they both radioed at the same time.

Ralph, stomping out a cigarette, started to radio that Roscoe had run out from between the houses across Elm toward Santa Monica Boulevard. Then he thought, Nah, and kept an eye out for Bob's truck. Bob and Cyndi backed in opposite directions out of the alley, Bob smashing a trash can in the process.

"He had to go west," Bob radioed to no one in particular. "Cyndi, head west on Randolph. I'll head west on Tecumseh. O'Connell, head west on Morgan and come north on Santa Monica. Over."

"Aye, aye, sir. And good luck to all of us," O'Connell replied. He was getting into this. He floored the accelerator and squealed south on Fifth Street, screamed around the turn and headed west on Morgan two blocks to Santa Monica, slammed on the brakes at the stop sign, and peeled out onto the thoroughfare. "I've got the point, sir!" he radioed.

All that car noise scared Roscoe, who headed back east toward Elm, clearing low fences and dodging between the houses. "O'Connell! Get back to Fifth between Tecumseh and Randolph."

"Taking the fifth, sir!" O'Connell replied, and squealed back toward where he had just come from. Bob crossed Elm on Tecumseh just a little ahead of Roscoe. Ralph was hiding behind a tree. Bob turned into the south end of the alley and almost slammed into Cyndi coming from the north. Roscoe was nowhere to be seen.

"This is stupid, sir. The dog knows we're chasing him. We're not going to catch him like this,' she said, mentally adding, And we're certainly not going to catch him on foot, thinking of Ralph and her own not-so-great physical condition. Even Ranger Bob was a little portly, though he still wore those tight pants and shirts.

As if reading her mind, Bob sucked in his gut. "He does the same thing every time. This time, I'll be on foot on Elm. You drive west, curl around, cut him off to the west, and run him back this way. Ralph and I'll grab him. Ralph, where are you," Bob radioed.

"Here, Bob," Ralph said from right behind him. Ralph had wandered down the alley to see what the other two were talking about. "O'Connell, where are you?"

"Still heading south on Fifth, sir. I'm almost to the Wal-Mart. Need anything?"

"Goddamn it, O'Connell, you're a mile away. Come back here, right now."

"I'll be working my way back to you, sir," O'Connell said, on key. Bob glared at the microphone. You can't depend on college kids, he thought. From now on, I'm just hiring professionals. "Go, Cyndi. Ralph, you're with me."

Cyndi did what she was supposed to do, Ralph and Bob did what they were supposed to do, Roscoe did what they expected him to do, except about a half block to the south from where the dogcatchers were stationed. They chased him over Fifth Street and lost him headed down the hill toward Fourth Street. They trudged back up the hill to see O'Connell arriving.

"Any luck, sir?" he asked.

"No. This time, we all sit in the alley between Fifth Street and Bauer's house. That dog'll want to come home. With four of us there, we'll catch him in that pinch point between the fences." And there they sat all night. Roscoe didn't think of Bauer's house as home just yet. He and his master were still sorting one another out. So he just hunkered down his gang in an old garage on Fourth Street and went to sleep.

Bob never did get any sleep. He sent the others home and commandeered one of the city trucks the next day, returning to stake out Bauer's house. Roscoe had already returned and was safe in the back yard. Fortunately, Mike worked at night and was home during the day. Otherwise, Bob might have just gone into the back yard and nabbed the dog.

It was standoff, and Bob didn't get much help from the neighborhood. This was the north end of town, and people didn't have much use for Animal Control. There were a lot of dogs that escaped in the North End, and Bob had put some in the city gas chamber a little early. Ranger Bob was intensely disliked. Now he was in the neighborhood on some mission, and the neighborhood smelled an opportunity to monkey wrench the unpopular city official. The word went from neighbor to neighbor, from backyard barbeque to the tavern two blocks away on the corner. They conspired. They found that about 5 p.m., Mike went to work. Soon after that, Roscoe ventured out. Soon after that, Bob and his stupid camoflage truck would arrive.

Bob and the dog would see one another about the same moment, and Bob would give chase. Roscoe would take off in any of several different directions with Bob in pursuit. People came out on porches and front lawns to see the Animal Control truck was speeding by. Roscoe would run by, and they'd cheer. Bob would drive by, and they'd boo. It was great fun.

Bob wasn't having any fun. He was being ridiculed and humiliated. He thought the dog was doing this on purpose, and at this point, he probably was right. Roscoe was having a lot more fun running this way and that along the streets and alleys than he would have cooped up in Bauer's backyard in the middle of winter.

Bob became a man possessed. He had the whole Animal Control Department working on catching Roscoe. No other part of town was getting served. People in the North End were starting to bring out lawn chairs and coolers to watch the late afternoon entertainment. Go dog go! they'd yell when Roscoe whizzed by. He went thataway, Asshole! they'd yell when Animal Control came by.

O'Connell started a pool among city employees to try and pick a date; (A) when Roscoe would be caught, or (B) when Ranger Bob would be hauled into the Public Safety director's office. After three weeks, there was $3,500 in the pot.

Mike was oblivious. He was new to the neighborhood, didn't speak to the Gulates or many other of his neighbors, went to work at 5 p.m. and came home after midnight to find his dog waiting in the backyard. Usually. He'd found the trench Roscoe had dug between the garage doors, and so did something he'd been meaning to do for a long time - pave the driveway to the alley. In fact, the back yard was beginning to look pretty good. New gate, reinforced fence, paved driveway, re-hung doors on the garage. He was kind of proud of himself, and thanked Roscoe for instigating all the repairs. "Sorry you can't get out anymore, but that's life, buddy."

Funny thing, Mike thought. When winter rolled around just after Zeke died, I was pretty depressed about, well, about everything. My job, Kay, this neighborhood. I don't feel quite so bad anymore. Roscoe just grinned and panted. He liked Mike.

Nobody liked Bob, and Bob was less happy than usual. He wasn't depressed, he was possessed. He couldn't catch Roscoe following the rules. Rules were made for the law-abiding, he thought. Criminals have no respect for the rules. That's why the public hires us to protect them. If the perpetrator can run across lawns, I can run across lawns. If the perp had no respect for private property, well, law enforcement couldn't stop at the Cambodian border when that's where the Viet Cong hid.

One evening, with Cyndi in the pinch point between the fences in the alley between Fifth and Elm, Bob finally caught Roscoe headed toward her. He cut up a driveway on Fifth and peeled after the dog, continuing over the end of the driveway and across a lawn before sliding into the alley and ending up right in front of Cyndi's truck.

"Where'd he go?" he asked.

"I never saw him," Cyndi replied.

Roscoe had this down pat. He'd go into the garage, jump up on the work bench, leap across to the table saw and out the garage window onto the woodpile leaning up against the outside garage wall, and then into some bushes between Bauer's side yard and Gulates'. Coming back home after he'd run with his gang, he'd head toward the pinch point in the alley and run right under the bumper of whatever truck was sitting there. Whoever was in the truck never saw him, and he was into the bushes, up the log pile, through the garage window and into the garage - safe at home!

For Bob, the end of the chase was driving over that lawn. O'Connell had it pegged almost to the hour. There was one hell of a fraternity party that weekend when he walked away from City Hall with $3,700 in cash for picking the exact day that Bob Branson got summoned to the office of Public Service Department Director Thomas M. Schuette, head of police, fire, emergency management and several other agencies, including Animal Control.

"Bob, what are you doing up there around Fifth and Randolph? I've got 16 written complaints from residents up there."

"There's a vicious dog loose up there, sir. Could be rabid. We're trying to catch it, is all," Bob replied.

"I checked, Bob. We don't have any bite cases up there. And I'm supposed to be notified of a rabies problem, which I have not been so notified. What the citizens up there tell me is you and your people have been running all over the neighborhood chasing some harmless pet, and I do mean all over the neighborhood. Mrs. Jankowski said you drove over her lawn, and she's sent the repair bill to the city."

"Sir," Bob began, only to be cut off.

"And you know what else I'm hearing? Animal complaints from other parts of the city aren't being answered at all. You've had Jolene Mueller's cat impounded down there for 14 days - four days longer than necessary - and she can't get hold of you or anyone else."

"About the lawn, sir. I was in hot pursuit. I was chasing the suspect dog," Bob explained, in his best pseudo-military manner.

"Hot pursuit? Are you nuts? You're not a police officer, and this isn't some criminal. It's a neighborhood dog, for Christ's sake. You don't drive across people's yards to catch a stray dog!" Schuette yelled.

Bob started to say something, but Schuette was far from finished. Picking up a piece of paper, he said, "You know what this is? This is a clip from The Times-News about what they're calling the Ididadog. You're making your department and the city a laughing stock. People are sitting out on lawn chairs, drinking beer, watching you chase a dumb animal.

Which of you is dumber? Haven't we got enough problems up in the North End without this stupidity?"

"Sir," Bob started again.

"Sir, nothing," Schuette cut him off again. "You're suspended for two weeks. You're to stay away from your office, you're to have no communication with any of the employees, as of right now. We'll be running a performance audit of your department while you are gone, because I am sick to death of getting complaints about Animal Control in this city. No respect for the citizens, dirty cages, the distemper outbreak last year, and this time, you have really gone off the deep end. You might want to consider resigning. If the audit comes out the way I think it will, we might have cause to terminate you. Now get out of here," Schuette finished.

News of the Ididadog eventually got to Mike. He was a something of a nerd by inclination and profession. He got his news from the Internet, and not the local newspaper. So he didn't read the newspaper until someone pointed one of the articles to him. He was partly amused at the thought of the entire resources of Animal Control being focused on his dog, and partly mortified at the thought of his dog out every night causing such mischief in the area.

Mike began to understand that even a dog can get lonely and bored. He decided right then and there that he'd take up an offer made by a couple friends at work to buy into some land down into the Ozarks. Not a big place - 530 acres - but a place where he could get away during his off days and let Roscoe run out some of that excess energy.

But he did wonder how Roscoe was getting out of the yard. A paw print in the sawdust on top of the table saw provided the key clue. Fine, Mike thought. He went inside, called work, left a message for Arnie that he was taking another personal day. At the end of that day, the two south facing windows on the garage had glass in them. Next Sunday, now knowing how to do it, the two north-facing windows in the garage would also be filled with glass, and the garage remodeling would be done.

"Thanks, boy," Mike said to Roscoe.

The following day at work, Arnie came over to Mike's desk. "We need to talk about your latest personal day," Arnie said, pronouncing the word "personal" as if it was a sex crime.

"I'm pretty busy right now, Arnie. Can't it wait?"

"No, it can't. This is the fourth time this has happened. You get personal days, but you're taking them at inconvenient times for me. We're going to agree on some rules here," Arnie said.

Mike almost said that the photos he was processing had to be downstairs in an hour. Mike would have much rather been a photographer for the magazine, but he had a talent for working with Adobe Photoshop. He could make mediocre pictures into gems. Of course, he also got stuck with developing film and processing wire photos and all that other non-creative stuff. It paid more than being a photographer; it just wasn't very interesting. Or much fun. It was a lot like being trapped in a fenced yard, Mike thought.

"Sure Arnie. Be right with you." Arnie walked away to get a cup of coffee, and Mike stored everything he'd been working on. It was 5:30, and the first deadline was 6:30. Mike had processed and moved four of the 17 pictures Composing needed. What would Roscoe do, he thought, as he cooled his heels in Arnie's office, waiting for his boss to return. He'd be cool, man.

Arnie returned about five minutes later and started in a long, one-sided dissertation that began with "Yes, I know what's in the contract, probably better than you" and progressed to "It takes more than one person to put this magazine out. There is no 'I' in team, you know" (But there is in 'cliché,' Mike thought) to "When you let your team members down, in my view, you let yourself down" to "Where is it that you want to go with this company, Mike."

That took a half an hour. "Where do I want to go with this company, Arnie? At this point in my career, I'd like to make enough money to enable me to get into a different line of work. There isn't a promotion on this floor that I would apply for, not one, not even your job," Mike said.

That engendered another lecture. Mike hardly paid any attention. He felt free. Arnie couldn't really fire him, or even discipline him as long as he did his job, and Mike did his job well. Arnie could transfer him, but now Arnie couldn't have any idea with what job Mike could be threatened. That was always the last resort for the company in dealing with a recalcitrant employee; send him or her to an unpleasant posting and hope they quit. Except now, Mike appeared to be immune to that treatment; he didn't like where he was, and he wouldn't like anywhere Arnie sent him.

At the moment, Arnie was just talking to kill time while he tried to think of some way to get to Mike Bauer, when Allison Washington knocked on the door. Washington was head of the photo department, and Arnie's boss. She walked in and looked at Mike. "Mike, what are you doing? Composing is screaming for those photos."

"Arnie wanted to talk to me," Mike said serenely. "I told him I was pretty busy. He said it couldn't wait."

"Arnie?"

"Allison, he didn't mention he was on deadline. Mike, get back to your desk."

Mike got up and left to Allison's words, "Don't you know when deadline is?," directed at Arnie. He could tell looking through Arnie's office window that the discussion was getting somewhat heated. Mike didn't care. He went back to work, did the best he could to catch up, although there was no way to hit the deadline at this point. And when his shift ended, he went home.

Where he found Roscoe sitting on the front porch. Mike didn't get mad. He didn't even wonder how Roscoe had gotten out this time. The man just sat down beside the dog, and the dog leaned against his master, sliding his eyeballs to the upper right corners of his eyes to gaze at his master with love and affection…and just a little bit of rebelliousness left in reserve.

"You want to go down to the farm this weekend, Pup? Maybe we can run some of this excess energy out of you, although you sure have taught me something. No matter what kind of fence they wrap around you, it's no excuse for not taking control of your life. No, sir," Mike said, and ruffled the fur on Roscoe's head. "Now, how did you get out this time?"

Mike never did figure this one out, but Roscoe had found a pile of wood left over from one of Mike's Roscoe-induced remodeling projects piled up against the garage wall. It was a one story garage with not much of a pitch on the roof. Roscoe leaped nimbly to the top of the scrap wood pile, bounced to the roof, crossed over the south side, jumped down on top of the firewood pile, and off into the neighborhood to run around with like-minded, four-footed escape artists. And this was spring, about the time the Gulates' purebred came back into heat.

It was only a couple days after Roscoe had renewed his acquaintance with his absent but not forgotten lover that Mike went down to the farm. Roscoe ran and ran and ran and eventually ran so far that he never came back. Mike looked for him for two days, and the following weekend, and the weekend after that. A local in the nearby town ventured the opinion that coyotes had lured Roscoe, an unfixed male, off into the woods and killed him.

"Them coyotes'll do that. They'll send a bitch coyote around t' your male, and your dog'll run off after that bitch. Then the males'll come out and kill 'im. Seen it happen, I have," the man said.

"You a coyote hunter?" Mike asked.

"That I am, and a purty good tracker. Name's Dick Smith."

"Well, Mr. Smith, I wonder if you couldn't come out to my place tomorrow. I'll show you where I last saw Roscoe, and maybe you can give me an idea what happened to him."

"Can do. You got the old Fliniau place, don't you? I'll see you bright and early," Smith said.

Smith did do an impressive job of trying to reconstruct where Roscoe might have gone, but the trail was three weeks old. Smith did find plenty of coyote sign, which didn't surprise Mike. He'd seen lots of coyotes while he was deer and turkey hunting. A couple things Smith did find surprised Mike; old wells. "You got, what? 500 acres here. There used to be six families living here on six different farms. Back then, a person din't need all this land t' support themselves. A few pigs, couple a cows, a lot of poachin' did for them jus fine. I'm guessin' if'n the coyotes din't git your dog, he fell down one of them wells; couldn't get out. Maybe drowned," Smith said, wrapping up the investigation.

Mike drove back to the city, thinking about his dog for all of the 150 miles. For some reason, he didn't feel bad, not as bad as he'd felt when Zeke died. Wonder why, Mike thought to himself.

Several weeks later, an angry Gulate was at his door. "Your goddamn dog has gotten our dog with pups again, and this is the last time that's going to happen. We're going to Animal Control right now," Anne almost yelped through the screen door, her voice cracking as she lost control.

"Do they look like Roscoe?" Mike asked innocently.

"Yes, they goddamn do, and you damn well know it. You're in deep shit, Mister. What are you going to do about it? We're talking real goddamn money here."

Mike was about to say, "Can I have one of the pups?," then had a better idea.

"Real money? Why should I pay you cause your dog had puppies? You can't prove it was Roscoe. You let your dog out almost every night. It could have been any dog, and you know it."

"Goddamn it, it was your goddamn dog. We do not let our dog out at night, you liar, and we'll take you to court if you don't pay, if you don't pay…" she turned and looked at Don. "How much does he have to pay, Don."

"$500."

"If you don't pay the goddamn $500," Brenda yelled.

"Can I ask you a question, Brenda?"

"What."

"Can you get through an entire sentence without saying 'goddamn'?"

"Fuck you," Brenda said.

"Well, that's a whole sentence," Mike said. "If you want to take me to court, go ahead. I'm not paying you $500. No way."

"There are ways to prove your dog is the goddamn father, you know. We'll spend as much money as it goddamn takes, and you'll end up paying it."

Mike stepped outside. Aggravate them a little more, he thought. That's how Roscoe got the dogcatcher.

"Sure there are ways, Anne. I just didn't think you and Don were smart enough to know that. But I don't think you'll spend the money. That's why you put up that cheap little fence instead of making a nice secure one. That's why your house looks like shit. That's why you're a disgrace to the neighborhood. Now get off my porch, and get off my property. Excuse me, my goddamn property."

They left, because this wasn't the Mike Bauer they used to know. This Mike Bauer was assertive and self-confident. Don had had his hands balled up into fists, expecting a fight, but Mike had been fearless, confident. Don didn't like that. Better let someone else take care of Bauer.

Animal Control was no help. The department had been taken over by a sane person. "Mrs. Gulate, I appreciate your disappointment in your, uh, litter, but this is really a civil matter between you and Mr. Bauer. If his dog is really running loose, we'll try and catch it, but that's the limit of our responsibility."

Anne started to say something, but the new director added, "If, as you say, you want to breed your dog for AKC registered pups, you'll need a special license to do that, and that activity is not allowed in that neighborhood. That whole area is zoned residential."

That shut Anne and Don up. They went next to a lawyer. "That'll be $500 to take the case, $120 in fees to file it, and $70 per hour," the lawyer said.

"And if we win?" Anne asked.

"We can ask the court to order him to pay all fees, plus damages. But I have to ask, are you absolutely sure that his dog impregnated yours?"

"There's no goddamn doubt," Anne said. "The pups look exactly like Roscoe, his dog, exactly. And his is the only dog in the neighborhood that's out every goddamn night."

"Fine, I'll take the case. This should be fun. A paternity test on a dog; that'll make the paper."

When the case came before Municipal Court, the first thing Mike had to deal with was a possible contempt of court citation. Judge Andy Briscoe was a down home, practical sort who didn't waste a lot of time on legalese, which was because he was not a lawyer. He was a lay judge appointed by the state because no lawyer wanted to take a job that only paid $70,000 a year. Briscoe figured if people were really serious about these lawsuits, they could appeal to the District Court. Otherwise, a lot of these petty matters could be settled at what Briscoe liked to describe as the lowest court in the land.

However, this Mr. Bauer had failed to produce his dog for tests.

"I can't produce my dog, your honor. He ran away at my farm, which is about 150 miles from here, about two months ago."

"Can you prove that? And don't call me your honor. Call me Judge Briscoe."

"Well, Judge, here's a note from a Mr. Dick Smith, who I hired to find Roscoe. You'll see he says in the note that we couldn't find him. And here's some ads I took out in the local paper down there. And I guess you could come over to my house right now and see that there's no dog there," Mike said.

Judge Briscoe looked a little perplexed. "Mr. Begwell," he said, addressing the Gulates' attorney. "Your clients only filed this case a month ago. Did they know Mr. Bauer's dog was missing, perhaps dead?"

"Mr. Bauer didn't volunteer that information, Judge Briscoe."

"Mr. Bauer, did you conceal this information?"

"No sir. Nobody asked me. All I told Don and Anne was that they couldn't prove anything, 'cause they let their dog run at night…"

"Objection," Begwell announced.

"Yes?" the judge asked.

"My clients aren't the defendants here. It's irrelevant whether Snookie gets out at night."

"Snookie?"

"Our godd…, our dog," Anne Gulate supplied.

"Mr. Bauer?"

"It's totally relevant, Judge Briscoe. This is a city of 50,000 people. Animal Control said there were 6,756 dog licenses issued last year. Of those, 106 were Australian shepherds or mixes. Their dog could have been impregnated by any of them."

"Mr. Begwell?"

"It's still irrelevant, Judge. The Gulates have a fenced back yard. Their dog is an AKC registered German shorthair. It is very valuable, as we'll show. There's is no way that dog can get out of that yard. And it hasn't."

"Mr. Bauer?"

"A dog can get out of a yard, believe me. They don't have that good a fence. I'd like to hear them swear under oath that their dog can't get out. Then I'd like to go over there and whistle, and we'll see what happens," Mike said.

"Mr. Begwell?"

"We will, in fact, swear under oath that our dog cannot get out of that yard. And we'll go over there right now and prove it. Will that satisfy Mr. Bauer? And then can we get on with our case?"

"Mr. Bauer?"

"Well, judge, here's the dog licenses for both dogs. You'll see they're close to the same size, except Snookie - and he couldn't help laughing at the name - Snookie is about 10 pounds heavier."

"I see that. So?"

"Well, if their dog can't get out of that yard, how could my dog have gotten in?"

This was a silence, Mike thought, that usually comes right before the credits start rolling on the TV screen.

"Mr. Begwell?"

"Judge Briscoe, some dogs are more adept at getting over or through fences, than others. Mr. Bauer's dog is known throughout the city…"

"Mr. Begwell," Judge Briscoe intervened, "I don't want to go off into whole other areas of speculation, only what can be proved. Mr. Bauer has asked a pertinent question, I am satisfied he can't produce his dog, and the court can't speculate on supernatural abilities. If your dog can't get out, it follows that his dog can't get in. If your dog did get out, there is no reason to believe that only Mr. Bauer's dog was the culprit. Anyone who lives in this city knows there's any number of dogs running loose on any given night. To paraphrase, Mr. Bauer's dog is innocent until you prove it's guilty."

Begwell tried some more arguments out on the judge, but Briscoe wasn't having any of it. After about 15 minutes, he ruled in favor of Bauer and assessed all costs to the Gulates, costs that included an estimate of what Bauer's time was worth defending himself.

Once Mike got that, he went to his favorite bar to celebrate. "Don't get drinks for the house, Schappe, but drinks for the bar."

"How much did they have to pay you?" Schappe asked.

"$600."

"Cool," Schappe said, and went to fill pitchers.

"So what happened after Briscoe ruled in your favor?" Mike's friend Dedecker asked.

"Don and Anne had this gigantic argument in the hall. He said something like, you wanted to do this, and you wanted to file this stupid lawsuit. Now we've spent over a thousand dollars, the story's in the paper, everybody's laughing at us. I'm beginning to think you're as stupid as everyone says you are."

"Don said that to his wife?"

"Not exactly. I'm cleaning up the language. The judge ordered the bailiff to remove them from the building."

"So you walk away with $600, and you didn't even have a lawyer." Dedecker said, shaking his head in wonderment.

"I'm not exactly free. If Roscoe shows up, they can reopen the case and get a DNA sample, which I have no doubt will show that Roscoe is the daddy," Mike said.

"But he's dead."

"I don't know that. I don't even believe that."

Dedecker looked a little confused. "I was wondering why you weren't all that upset when your dog disappeared, not like when Zeke died. What's up with that? Why didn't, you know, this amazing dog find his way back home, or at least to the farmhouse?" he asked.

"I've thought about that. I think Roscoe stayed around my place as long as he was needed, then went somewhere else. He didn't really like my yard. After he'd been to the country a few times, I think he decided he liked the freedom."

"I think he's dead, Mike. I think he fell down one of those wells, or he got killed by coyotes. I think that Dick Smith hit it right on the head. I know you don't want to hear that, but that's reality," Dedecker said.

"I don't think that, DD. Suppose he got lured out by a female coyote and got surrounded by five or six hungry males. Suppose he fell down a well and had to swim around in ten feet of water with no way out. Think about it. He escaped from his first owners, who were jerks. He escaped from my yard, over and over and over again. He escaped from the dog pound. He escaped five or six dogcatchers chasing him night and day. He escaped responsibility for raising his kids, he escaped the long arm of the law. You think escaping from a well with a bunch of howling coyotes up top was any problem for him? Do you?"

Dedecker mulled that over for a while. "You might be right," he said. "Hear you're a photographer again, with weekends off. You taking Kay to the ball game Saturday?"

"Nah. Think I'll give Robbie a call. I need a change of scenery," Mike said, taking a long, appreciative drink of his beer.

Requiem For A Messiah

Tancredus Wilhelm Baxter absently patted the hood of the battered GMC pickup that didn't seem to be as elegant a vehicle as would be required by someone with such an imposing name. As if in recognition of that fact, Tancredus Wilhelm Baxter went by the name of Tank, as befitted his role as a lineman on a high school team that almost, but didn't quite win the state championship lo these many years ago. That was back when his eyes were better, his hair was thick, knees not failing and mind was quick. Now, he had to worry about his prostate and polyps on the inside of his large intestine. He had to keep an eye on those suspicious spots on his arms and face. His total medical supply bill used to consist of a bottle of aspirin, disinfectant and Band-Aids. Now, he spent $150 a month on prescription medicine. But he felt good this morning, good and fit.

Tank had kept himself fit by partaking of such activities as he planned today. The start of that activity was a trail that led off into the yellowing aspens and lodgepole pines of the western forests just below the Continental Divide. That was the trail that would lead him to Bear Mountain.

"Aptly named," he thought, "It's going to be a bear." He'd been planning on climbing the mountain for the ten years he'd lived out here. Bear Mountain rose 12,180 feet above sea level, which translated to 2,400 feet above the trail on which Tank stood.

This wouldn't be a technical climb with ropes and belays and all that. Tank didn't know how to do that, and didn't want to know how to do that. His rule was that he didn't climb any mountain Rex couldn't climb. Rex looked up at him and appreciatively wagged his tale as if to reinforce the understanding he had with his master, and that was that his master didn't leave him behind.

When Tank had been suicidal, one of only a few influences that kept him from walking off into the woods and quietly freezing to death was the knowledge that his dogs, and this one in particular, would never be adopted. Rex was hyperactive, and big. Not many people would want a hyperactive lummox in their homes. The dog had, in fact, been eight days beyond the Humane Society's kill date when Tank had found him at the pound. It was just no one at the shelter could bring themselves to slip the Big Needle to the big, good-natured galoot.

The workers at the pound had only a taste of the loyalty and devotion Rex was capable of giving to the right human. And Tank believed that when a bond was established between a man and a dog, some rules applied. One of those was that you never left the dog behind, if you could help it, even in death. Theoretically, the dog shouldn't leave the master behind either, even in death. But it was a biological fact of life that dogs didn't live as long as humans.

And dogs don't have much in the way of choices. They're kind of stuck with whatever human they've got, and if that human puts them in harm's way, well, that's a dog's fate. Tank thought he had lost Rex more than once to misadventure, but the dog seemed to be blessed. He never even got sick.

"Everyone else left us behind, huh, Rex," Tank said, absently patting the car hood again, thinking the dog rule probably didn't apply to motor vehicles. He was about to leave Surefoot behind, for the day anyway. Surefoot had ten years and 299,000 miles on it - the best vehicle Tank had ever owned. He had driven it all over the Rocky Mountains, ever since moving out West. He had developed a possibly unnatural affection for it.

"Why is that?" a friend had asked one night, over a couple of beers, or maybe more than a couple of beers.

"Well, let me tell you a story. I was driving back from a basketball game in some town I don't remember, taking the back roads. This one highway took me along the Colorado River, along a really huge gorge. They call it the Trough Road, except this was maybe one of the biggest and deepest troughs on earth. It's a really pretty drive, but I couldn't exactly see down into the gorge from the main road. So I saw this little dirt road leading off the main road down toward the river.

"That road led to another road, hardly more than two ruts, that led right to the gorge, or at least it looked that way. I followed that. It led right to a cliff. Great view, but I couldn't turn around. I had to back up a quarter mile before I could get going in the right direction. Then, it was so steep I didn't know if Surefoot could pull the hill or not.

"I hadn't realized it, but I was about six miles from the Trough Road. And only few cars use that highway, at least at that time of year."

"So what's the big deal? You did some 4-wheeling," the friend observed.

"That wasn't it. I got back to town okay, ate, went to sleep. The next day, I got up to take the dogs for a walk, and the truck goes 10 feet and dies. Found out later the CPU went out. Do you know what kind of deep caca I would have been in if the CPU had gone out at that cliff? That truck has never stranded me, anywhere. It's got the original engine, original transmission. It's been great," Tank said.

"Plus, you don't have payments. Plus, you didn't have to pay sales tax on a new car. Plus, you pay almost nothing in property taxes," the friend observed.

"Yep, all that too," Tank agreed.

"Good thing you don't care what it looks like," came the zinger from his buddy.

"You look fine," Tank said to the truck sitting at the trailhead. He usually locked the car up when he went hiking because of all the stuff he left in it. Nobody'd be dumb enough to steal the actual car. This vehicle was in such a state that the items inside the truck were worth more than the truck.

He'd taken all that stuff out - spotlight, electric tire pump, gloves, tools, tow strap, shovel, axe, those kinds of things. Tank had the feeling Surefoot wasn't going to make 300,000 miles, so in case the truck experienced its final breakdown, he wanted to be able to walk away without having to worry about 15 or 20 items of miscellaneous equipment.

He'd had that same feeling about Bill the Beagle, that Bill wasn't going to make 300,000 miles, or 2.1 million in dog miles. Bill came with Tank, his wife, three other dogs and two cats when they moved out West from Missouri. Bill hadn't liked it out here. The beagle had been a fair rabbit dog - hell on cottontails. But the dog had taken one look at a western jackrabbit, which must have looked like a bunny on steroids, and wouldn't ever hunt again.

And Bill was a little guy, spoiled fat by his ex-wife. When the wife abandoned the whole family, including Bill, the little beagle seemed to sink into himself. Tank could still get the dog's attention with (a) food, (b) more food, and (c) a place by the fire. But the beagle's health slowly deteriorated until Tank took him in for the Big Needle. He thought it was a relief for them both when it was done.

Surefoot had gotten him across the county, up the gravel road, up the dirt road, and then up the four-wheel drive road to this particular spot without overheating too much. The truck was dripping oil onto the dirt and smelled like burned transmission fluid, but it had gotten them this far.

Tank stopped leaning on the hood and inventoried his equipment again. It was 7 a.m., and he had all day. But he wasn't planning on spending the night, so he'd brought the day pack for him and the light dogpack for Rex. The dog would be carrying water and dog biscuits only.

Tank had water, candy bars, fruit juice, one camera, windbreaker, long-sleeved shirt, hunting knife, snub-nosed .38, and various other small items - map, matches, compass. He didn't think he could possibly get into a situation where he might need all those items, but you never knew what could happen in a wilderness area. The people you read about in the paper were those who hadn't brought all that little, inconvenient to carry stuff.

They didn't realize they shared the woods with moose, elk, deer, bears, mountain lions, leaning snags, loose rocks, slippery stream beds, lightning, unpredictable weather and several other conditions to which flatlanders paid little attention. He hadn't himself until he'd lived up here a few years.

"Remember that doofus who got lost two miles from camp," Tank said to Rex, as if Rex read the paper. "Ended up walking 17 miles over the Continental Divide carrying a rifle and all that elk hunting gear. They found him at a ski resort, hypothermic, almost dead, but still stupid."

Rex looked up at him as if he understood, but also as if he understood that his particular human could never make such an extended error in judgment. Dogs were lucky in that they got to live with their gods, interact with them, talk to them, see them in the flesh every day.

"And you're saying that if this fellow would have had a dog with him, he could have curled up with the dog and been at least partly safe from the cold," Tank said, looking at Rex, who looked back as if in agreement with that thought, and also with the premise that if every human had a dog, many of the extended errors recorded in world history would never have been made.

"Dogs' thoughts are either extremely shallow, or extremely deep," Tank thought. He looked at Surefoot one more time, sighed, and turned toward the trail. Rex took his customary position about 30 feet ahead, and they were off.

This was one part of hiking that he didn't like. He'd have to walk four miles to get to the base of Bear Mountain, the fun part of the hike. And this particular trail went up 400 feet, then back down, across a stream, then back up again. Tank hated giving up altitude he had already gained. Of course, there were several mountains in the area he could climb - had climbed - by just driving to the base. But there were usually other people also climbing those mountains.

"If the mountains were homeowners, they'd be complaining about the traffic," Tank thought. He didn't hike at all in national parks anymore. Too many rules. For instance, Rex would have to be on a leash. Rex hated leashes. The dog was born to run in the mountains, and would probably die doing that. The dog certainly had come close to death more than once. The one time Tank had been sure Rex was dead was when the dog got sucked into an irrigation pipe.

The Michigan Ditch ran six miles around the contours of the highest mountains in the county to divert water to the flatlands to the east. The ditch was eight feet wide, six feet deep and full of spring runoff. The Water Authority had been enclosing the ditch with six-foot diameter culverts to keep landslides from blocking the flow. Rex had jumped into the ditch right in front of one of those culverts.

He'd gotten sucked in butt first, frantically trying to swim upstream. The last Tank thought he'd ever see of his dog was his goofy face disappearing into the darkness of the pipe, so full that only six inches of air was available at the top. Tank ran to the downstream end of the 200-yard long pipe. And waited, and waited. Rex was a big, strong dog, and Tank imagined that he was still trying to swim upstream, so he called to him, and whistled.

Eventually, after what seemed the longest time, Rex popped out of the far end, crawled up on the shore, shook himself off, looked at Tank as if to say, "What the Hell was that!!?"

"That was the rinse cycle, big dog. That was the rinse cycle," Tank had said, so full of relief that he'd almost cried.

Tank laughed softly at the memory, then realized he'd walked almost two miles without much noticing where he was. What yanked him out of his reverie was an awful smell wafting down on the wind that told Tank that a bear was in the area. Tank wasn't worried for himself; this was black bear country, and those bears, unlike their grizzly cousins to the northwest, usually avoided humans. They were not averse, however, to taking a dog.

Rex was 110 pounds and very strong, but also possessed of the IQ of a Coleman lantern. The dog had a tendency to charge everything he encountered head on. He never bit anyone, but some stranger on the receiving end of a charge that tended to end inches from the crotch wouldn't know that. Rex had never run into a bear. "Although he did have that confrontation with the moose," Tank recalled.

That was one animal that hadn't fled at Rex's charge, and after avoiding a kick, Rex had come running back to Tank as if to ask what was going on with this particular beast. When the moose began eyeballing Tank, he'd decided both of them had better get out of the area.

Now, with a bear nearby, he made sure he knew where the gun was, and looked around for Rex. He whistled, knowing that Rex would hear, and ignore the whistle for a few moments as if the sound took a minute or two to traverse the distance between the ear and the brain.

Tank whistled again, and was rewarded by a familiar tread in the woods that told him Rex was running back to him. "Good dog," Tank said, scratching his head. "Trail, Rex," and the dog recognized the command to stay on the clear trail and returned to his position 30 yards ahead.

Part of Tank stayed alert, looking around for the bear. Part of him dropped into reverie again. He'd come out to the West with a wife, four dogs, and two cats. He'd also had two parents who had helped him set up his business. Now he had no wife, no parents, no cat and one surviving dog. His wife had taken one dog and one cat.

The remaining cat had hung around for five years. Tank left food out for the feline, maintained a warm place for it to sleep, but otherwise ignored it. He associated the cat with his ex-wife, and he was trying to forget everything about his ex-wife. Now, he couldn't remember the cat's name. This was disturbing, because Tank's dad had had Alzheimer's disease. That was an awful experience for the whole family, and a son who had loved, admired and respected his father had hated seeing that parent deteriorate into someone who could not be loved, or admired, or respected.

Tank had realized he'd forgotten the cat's name about a month ago, and had devoted more than a few hours while driving to trying to remember the cat's name. Surefoot's radio didn't work, so it was as good a means as any to pass the time on long, empty highways.

The West is hard on cats. A good, mean, fully-clawed feline was good for keeping rats and mice out of the barns, but most ended up as coyote sausage. Coyotes might be the most adaptable animal in America,

Tank thought. I talked to a rancher who said he shoots about 25 a summer, and the population never seems to change. You find them all over the place, on the prairie, in the woods, in suburbs even, munching on cats and small dogs.

That had almost been Bill the Beagle's fate. One day, Tank heard Bill yowling like he was on a rabbit's trail. Except Bill didn't hunt anymore. Tank went running toward the sound just in time to find a pack of coyotes closing in on the little beagle. The coyotes fled when Tank arrived, but he spent the next few days doctoring puncture wounds on Bill's butt.

He'd liked that little beagle. He'd known the dog wasn't going to make another Christmas in the same way he knew that Surefoot the truck wasn't going to make it to 300,000 miles. The little brown and black dog had kind of faded into old age until he'd looked up at Tank one morning. The message in those rheumy eyes was unmistakable; "It's time, Tank." The man had wrapped the dog up in Bill's blanket and buried him deep in the yard. Six feet down was the depth you went in the West to avoid freezing. Bill had never liked the cold. Bill was a Missouri dog, and his favorite place in the high country of the West during the winter had been curled up close to the wood burning stove. Tank buried him deep enough so that he wouldn't be cold, and wrapped him up in the blanket just for some added insulation.

Tank whirled at the sound and looked back down the trail, a sound that had yanked him back into a real time and place. There was no mistaking the faint sound of a large animal's paw hitting the ground close by. But in this case, it was Rex. The dog had a penchant for chasing squirrels. Thirty yards ahead on a narrow trail coiling through thick pine woods, Tank hadn't seen him take off, deep in thought as he was. Rex ran by, and Tank stepped aside to avoid being reverse knee-capped by the passing dog who was totally oblivious to the fact that he was carrying packs that stuck out four inches on either side.

Tank hadn't even recalled snatching the .38 into his hand. As he put it back in the holster, he tried again to recall the name of that damn cat. It's old age. The memory goes along with everything else - the eyesight, the knees, the wind, the reaction time, the tautness of skin, the hearing, the prostate or whatever it was that meant he couldn't sleep the whole night through without rising at least once to go to the bathroom. And memory. Art Jones had told him that he had the same problem.

"My short-term memory is getting so bad, I can hide my own Easter eggs," Jones had said.

You've got to fight this aging all the way, Tank thought. So he indulged in such activities as long, hard hikes up mountains. And as he traipsed on down the boring part of the trail, he tried to think of all the cat names he had ever heard. He knew if the name came up, or if someone mentioned it to him, he'd know. Frisky. Boots. Blackie. Mittens. Clawed. Star. Cuddles. Dusty. Stripe. Tiger. Ferd. And a hundred others. But he couldn't for the life of him conjure up that cat's name. It had apparently passed entirely from his memory.

So he came to the stream below Bear Mountain without having much noticed the four-mile trek. Good trick, he thought. He could do that on any trail that didn't catch his interest. Could even do it driving down long, monotonous stretches of highway. In fact, he thought, more people ought to do that - give their brain some exercise by turning off the radio, or the TV for five or six hours. See what thoughts are produced by that suddenly undistracted brain.

Rex ran up and lowered himself in the stream as he drank deeply from some of the cleanest water in America. Tank took off his boots and socks to wade across the stream. He probably could have found a crossing, but he had this permanent spot of athlete's foot on the sole of his left foot. Couldn't get rid of it by any means other than wading in a mountain stream. The fungus would eventually come back, but a mountain stream could cure it for a few weeks. Strangest thing. He had to rub the sole across a mossy rock, and let the foot soak for a while. That did it. When he completed the therapy, he crossed the stream, put his socks and boots back on, and the itch that was a bitch was now the itch that was history.

As if to help out, Rex burst from the stream, ran up next to his master and shook exuberantly. Thanks for the shower, Rexor, Tank thought, and gazed up at Bear Mountain.

This was the interesting part of the hike. The main trail continued on to the north where it intersected with other trails headed west up to the Continental Divide. One of those trails started at the point where Tank was, at the moment, standing. Bear Mountain rose straight to the northwest, sticking abruptly out of the surrounding rising green forest like a hitchhiker's pink thumb sticking out of a green glove.

The peak was about 2,000 feet above where Tank stood. The interesting aspect of the peak was that it was separated from the ridge that connected it with the Divide by a deep gorge, almost a crack in the long, undulating ridge line. What intrigued Tank was that the crack cut off easy access to the peak from the western approach. That approach would have been easiest.

That didn't mean the mountain had never been climbed at that point, but it meant it hadn't been climbed very often. Your average touristas and day-hikers would take one of the two marked trails. Neither went up Bear Mountain. Some of the more adventurous would climb up to the shoulders of the peak to get a view from above the forest. But climbing the peak from the eastern approach would be something not many people would do. In addition, it was something not many people would do this time of year. It was after Labor Day, which cut way down on the number of touristas, and it was getting cold.

Tank could see a way up to the top for him and his dog. It was a way he had spotted before, as he hiked this area a lot. This climb, though, he'd never done, almost as if he was saving it for last. He shook that thought off and started through the woods straight to the northwest and began the assault. Rex, lacking a trail for guidance, simply ran in large circles around Tank as the man made his way through the timber and fallen logs.

This part of the forest was dry, so dry that the Forest Service had banned campfires, most kinds of gas lanterns and stoves and even smoking in the forest. The bed of the forest had a dusty, crackling feel to it as if even a sufficiently harsh word would ignite a conflagration. A novice couldn't tell if the pine trees were thirsty or not, but Tank could tell. The bark beetles were having their way with the normally resistant pines and spruces, and many of the trees that were sporting green needles this fall would be wearing red tops next summer.

Tank didn't know if he wanted to be around to see that or not. This part of the eastern slope of the Divide had been the last place that had received good water. Without about 400 inches of snow this winter, this part of the forest would lie naked and vulnerable to the next lightning strike, like a mongrel dog with its neck stretched out below the alpha male's shining teeth.

But for now, this was fun. Tank didn't smoke, didn't need a campfire, and would be happy, weary, and driving home at dusk. Not that anyone was waiting at home. That role used to be Fronck's. His ex-wife had given the dog that awful name for some unknown reason that, for lack of a better explanation, she said sounded right.

Tank called him Frank, and after Jez had left him, tried to expunge the Fronck moniker from the dog's memory. Fronck hadn't cared. Fronck had been abandoned and beaten and caged and generally abused most of his little dog's life. Jez had saved him from being dumped on a highway in the middle of February, and then left him without a thought to go live with a derelict cowboy.

Nobody would ever adopt Fronck again, Tank had thought. He was half pit bull, so most pounds in the U.S. wouldn't take him. Plus, Fronck had this habit of biting Tank's customers when he had the chance. He'd never done that before, but it was like the dog was looking for some sort of job to pay Tank back for being so kind to him. Defending the turf was the only thing he knew how to do. The dog was too arthritic to carry a pack, or even accompany his master on longer hikes, though the dog clearly wanted to.

Tank and Rex would take off on a hike, and Fronck would be sitting at the fence gate with his nose pressed through the space between the gate and its supporting post. I can do what Rex can do, his eyes seemed to say. But he couldn't. Fronck was all stove up from beatings and dog fights.

It broke Tank's heart to leave him behind, but he was rewarded by a furiously beating tail whenever he returned home. Fronck had been abandoned by everyone in his short life except Tank. He'd promised the little half breed that he'd never be left alone again. Tank didn't consider himself a superstitious individual, nor much of a science fiction buff, but after he'd had that little talk with Fronck, the human knew he'd never die before Fronck.

That was a form of abandoning the dog, dying on him. If there was any justice in life, dog and man would die at exactly the same moment. It's sad and unfair that a dog should pass and the man remain, or that the man should pass and leave the dog mourning at the odor of his grave.

But of course, dogs don't have the life span of humans, and Fronck had passed before Tank. But he didn't pass alone. He died in the arms of his master, probably believing that the needle entering his leg would end the pain and the torment. And it did.

Tank shook off the memory. The sadness was still there, but the death of dogs didn't have the long-term emotional impact of the loss of a wife whom he'd loved, or of his father, or of his mother. Two years ago, after such a hike, he had have made sure he was at a phone at 5 p.m. That would be 7 p.m. in North Carolina, and Mom would be expecting him to call. No hurry today. Dad had died first, then Mom.

Well, Tank thought, I can still believe Mom and Dad are up there. As long as I hold a deep and clear memory of them, they're there. And Mom loved to get pictures from little excursions like this.

"Why Tank,' she'd exclaim on the phone. "Did you really climb up to the top of this? What a sight that must have been, what a sight." And she'd always ask about Rex. She'd never ask about the other dogs. Even Dad, sinking into the mental morass of Alzheimer's, had always asked about Rex. And Mom, in the last months of her life, usually in a daze induced by the impact of cancer drugs, had always asked about Rex.

Tank could hear Rex careening about the dry woods. He could see evidence of his recent passage in the hanging dust of the midmorning air. The eastern slope below Bear Mountain was sheltered from the nearly constant western wind that hit the Divide and scoured the valley below. On this sheltered side, in the autumn sun, it was peaceful and almost warm.

And steep. Tank had come to the end of the pines and onto the treacherous rock scree formed by the mountain shedding its granite skin season after season. The southeastern face of the peak rose sharp and clean against the impossibly blue sky. Tank wouldn't be going that way.

What had once been a solid core of granite sticking out of the foothills had eroded to a conical peak that was fractured and broken by geologic ages. By just climbing around some boulders and cutting straight in toward the heart of the peak, Tank had a wide swath of rough path up to what looked like a healthy grove of limber pine. Tank loved limber pine. He hadn't grown up in the West; he'd grown up in the hardwood forests of Missouri. There wasn't a lot he regretted about leaving that part of the country, but he did miss those gnarly old oak trees and other hardwoods in the hidden areas of the hill country of the southern part of the state.

Limber pines, he imagined, were a cross between the oaks and evergreens. Limber pines were actually pines that had evolved to resist the wind. They sat low and solid to the ground, putting out thick branches that looked like the muscular arms of a sylvan weight lifter. To live on the high side of a mountain, exposed to 60 mph winds and temperatures reaching 60 degrees below zero required a tough composition.

This particular grove looked remarkably healthy given its exposed position and the drought. Supernaturally healthy, Tank thought. He sat down on a bent branch that provided a surprisingly comfortable seat and looked around at the grove. Rex trotted up and sat down beside him, looking up expectantly.

Distracted by that, Tank said, "I don't know buddy. We've only got three quarts of water, and probably no streams up here. We probably ought to wait." That was hard to do, though. The little grove occupied a shelf of about an acre in area ending at a sheer cliff towering over that trail intersection where Tank had stood about an hour earlier. The view was something that maybe only one half of one half of one percent of all the people who had ever lived in America would ever see.

The sun smiled down from high in the southeast, and no breeze disturbed the tranquility of the grove. Rex groaned almost noiselessly in contentment, and Tank felt his eyes grow heavy. He was 60 years old. He'd just hiked four miles at above 10,000 feet, and then climbed an additional 800 feet or so to this little grove. Just getting back to the car would give him more exercise than most of his fellow citizens would get in a month. His knee throbbed a little. Some delightful ham and cheese sandwiches and a cool drink of water awaited in the packs.

"No, buddy, we're not going to do that. We may never come back this way again, and I'm going to climb this peak while I'm here. I'm not going to rest, fall asleep, and wake up to find we've run out of time. Onward and upward, brave pup," Tank exclaimed, realizing he had probably read too many stories about King Arthur as a child, but added, "We may never pass this way again."

As he scoped out the next stage of the climb, he wondered if those books he read under the covers by flashlight (after his mother had told him to go to sleep) had influenced his life in any way. He hadn't exactly been a knight in shining armor, but he had, all in all, lived a virtuous life. I've never killed anyone, he thought, never even really hurt anyone. I've never cheated anyone out of any money. I've certainly given a lot away. When he'd moved out West, Jez had wanted to pack everything they owned into the trucks.

"What am I going to do with golf clubs where we're going?" he'd asked.

"Then we can sell them," she'd said. Jez was one of those people who would never have enough money. If she got $200 a week, she'd spend $210. If she got $2 million a week, she'd spend $2,100,000.

Tank wasn't that into building up a huge bank account, although he could have. At the time they decided to move west, he'd been making $80,000 a year and saving about a quarter of it just for lack of anything to spend it on. He didn't need the $50 the golf clubs might bring.

"How 'bout this," he suggested. "Let's have a party. Let's invite all our friends, and give them this stuff we don't need."

She'd been insistent. If we couldn't take it, sell it. "We're going to need the money," she'd said, although they'd had plenty. Actually, he thought, he'd had plenty. She'd never contributed a dime to the marriage. He hadn't cared. As long as they both had enough to live comfortably, that was sufficient.

The way he'd finally persuaded her to give up the clubs, and the portable air-conditioner, and the lawn mower, and weed trimmer, and extra refrigerator and TV, and all the other stuff filling a 2,000-square-foot home that wouldn't fit in a 14 by 70 foot mobile home was to say, "Hey, honey. If we give all this stuff away, I'll bet they'll help us load the trucks."

They would have helped anyway. They were actual friends. Tank hadn't completely lost touch with them in the ten years he'd been out West, but they'd all moved on. 1,000 miles of separation wears on friendships. You lose that thread of commonality you have when you spend a lot of time together. Absence doesn't make the heart grow fonder, it makes the heart go founder.

This seemed to take him to higher planes of thought as it took him to higher elevations. The rarefied air, he mused. And rarefied air it was. He could move about 100 feet at a time, then had to pause to catch his breath. Rex kept running up ahead and looking back as if to say, "Come on! There is more stuff up here. Come on!"

Dogs are rude, he thought, but started up again. He was now looking down on what he'd thought of as the Tranquil Grove of limber pines. Tranquil, as if some gentle person was buried there and true friends maintained the site. True friends being the trees, I guess, then wondered what produced that thought.

The cliff at the edge of that grove followed the line of the ridge. Tank stayed far from the edge. He had enough sense not to go near the crumbly rim, but he was sure Rex lacked any sense of the danger that cliff presented. The rock around the rim was old and fractured. A look at the boulder piles and scree at the bottom of the cliff presented ample evidence that it was eroding away in large chunks.

Tank bore to the right. That side of the ridge also fell away to the valley below, but not at anything like the near 90-degree face of the cliff.

Between the slope to the right and the cliff to the left was about 100 yards of ridge top heading up toward the peak. Tank and Rex followed it until they got to a grove of trees that looked as if it had endured repeated micro bursts of high winds. The twisted trunks and bent branches spoke silently of howling death and lost chances.

Lost chances? Where did that come from, Tank thought. Maybe because this looks like such a sad place. These trees aren't five feet tall, yet look like they might be 200 years old. Their branches look like limbs that had broken and then healed badly. What would it take to survive in this environment with its high winds, temperatures of 60 below, drought, short summers and long winters. He shivered at the thought. Who would be buried here? These little groves are like old cemeteries with big, mature trees. Maybe someone who lacked the warmth of human kindness in his life, or her life, and froze to death here. The trees grew up to shelter the grave.

Lost chances. I took almost every chance that came along. I stuck with everything to the end, to the bitter end in the case of Jez. And to the bitter end with a lot of other things, like that real estate partnership. Everyone else had gotten out, but he'd stuck with his partner right up to the point where the partner filed for bankruptcy without mentioning it to Tank. I've got bad karma, and I don't know why, he thought.

He reached down to scratch Rex's head without even thinking. Or even looking. Tank had just known Rex would be there next to him at that instant.

Rex moved in utter silence through the tough grass at that altitude, but the man and dog were so close that they anticipated one another's moves. Rex at this moment was anticipating that Tank would open one of the water bottles, and Tank did, pouring the dog's portion into his upturned hat. Rex lapped it up eagerly while Tank pulled out one of the sandwiches and broke it in two.

"I weigh 210; you weigh 110. You should only get a third," Tank told the dog. The dog ignored him, gulped down the offered half, then stared longingly at Tank as the man leisurely consumed the remaining half.

"Let's get out of here, Rexor. That peak is an hour away, at least," Tank said. Besides, the Blasted Grove made him uneasy for some reason. He imagined one of those tortured branches reaching out and grabbing him, pulling him with implacable force to squeeze all moisture and nutrients out of his crushed body so the fluids could feed the starving roots.

Rex looked at the man as if Tank had gone goofy. That was kind of a putrid image, Tank thought. If Tranquil Grove was the grave of a gentle soul, what manner of debased soul had polluted this patch of rank vegetation. Maybe it wasn't a polluted soul; maybe it was a lost chance, a decision made, then regretted, too late.

The ancient Greeks had legends that supposed men or women had turned into animals, or constellations, or a tree. A laurel tree, in one instance. Tank tried to think of the characters in that particular legend; a boy or a girl running from an ardent lover and praying to the gods for escape. The gods had answered, turning the girl/boy into an untouchable laurel tree. A not very famous legend, but I should know the name of the protagonist. I should also know the name of the damn cat. So what poor soul prompted the growth of this grove? Some powerful being who failed in some great project, perhaps.

There was, of course, no answer to that, or at least no possible answer to a question raised by an overactive imagination. The solution was to just leave, and he followed the narrowing ridge top toward the looming crag. The sun was almost directly overhead now; the sky was clear and blue. It was a beautiful day. Man and dog climbed higher.

At the base of the peak, Tank paused. The rule was: don't climb anything that Rex couldn't climb. That accomplished two things. It probably saved Rex, who would follow Tank wherever he went. Dogs aren't good climbers, at least most of them weren't. Second, the rule kept Tank from trying to climb cliffs beyond his own ability. And he could blame his reluctance (fear?) on the dog.

So he looked around for a proper path. From further below, he thought he'd seen a good route, but topography seems to change when you get closer to the object you want to traverse. So Tank walked first one way, then another around the base until he found a route both he and the dog could negotiate.

This was the best part of the hike. A path seemed to go straight into the peak, then up and sort of around and through some minor outcroppings. He could go up to the peak fairly easily without much climbing, which meant Rex could go too. And the view from the top was astounding; it always was.

He could see the Blasted Grove not too far below, but looking rather model trainish from this height. He could also make out the Tranquil Grove way down below, and looking like an aerial photograph was Fungus Killer Creek way, way down below. Awesome, he thought.

"Quite a view, isn't it?"

Tank jerked around and saw a man sitting not 20 feet away on one of the rock outcroppings. The man was dressed much like he was - jeans, heavy shirt, beat up hat, hiking boots, suspenders and belt hung with various implements peculiar to hikers. None of that which immediately met the eye would have startled Tank under ordinary circumstances except for the fact that the man was about 15 feet tall and about five feet wide.

"Feel free to be startled," the giant said.

"Color me startled," Tank said, and sat down heavily on a handy boulder. "What the hell are you?"

"The word 'hell' is a little inappropriate in this case. I am what you would call an angel, a celestial being, a messenger of God," the giant said, and then sat back against his own boulder as if waiting for Tank's reaction to that bit of news. Tank didn't have any reaction; he just sat and stared at what appeared to be a 15-foot-tall yuppie hiker.

Seeing no immediate response, the giant continued, "Should you wish to address me, my name is Michael. You are undoubtedly wondering if my tale is truth, which is why I come to you as a being twice as tall as is the norm in a human. I chose to meet you here because it is unlikely we will be disturbed by any other humans." Michael seemed about to continue, but Tank interrupted.

"What do you want?" he asked.

"Ah, Tank, always cutting past the irrelevant and moving directly to the point. Most people would ask for some sort of proof, some miracle. Money, perhaps? You do need a new truck. The return of your ex-wife, this time in a more loving character? The return of Fronck, in the fullness of health? 20-20 vision? None of this? It is perfectly in character for you not to want such a wish. You have earned everything you have, you have never taken a dime of charity in your life, you do not play the lottery, you have never been on welfare, yet you have given away thousands of dollars," Michael mused aloud.

"You know a lot about my life," Tank observed.

"I know everything about your life," Michael responded. "You have lived a life of good examples. You do not lie, you do not cheat, you do not steal. You are what used to be called a man of honor. You keep your promises, you pay your debts, you have a set of principles, and you do not vacillate from those principles. I can see a couple of scars on you that mark the results of such integrity."

"You make me sound perfect. I'm not," Tank said.

"We know you are not. Nobody is, or was," Michael agreed.

"Not even Jesus?"

"Not even Jesus, and I knew him. I could tell you some stories," Michael said, shaking his large head.

Tank was shaking his head too, wondering if he'd fallen off the jagged peak and hit his head. He'd never done hard drugs, but he imagined this would be something like an LSD flashback. Or a dream. Tank thought perhaps he'd dozed off back in the Tranquil Grove and was dreaming the continuation of his climb. He'd certainly had dreams that had seemed incredibly realistic. They'd seemed incredibly realistic upon waking, that is. This dream seemed to be continuing.

"You have not suffered a head injury, you are not experiencing a drug induced flashback - although you accidentally did do hard drugs that one time - and you are not dreaming," Michael said, going through Tank's attempts at a logical explanation in perfect order. And there were very, very, very few people on earth who knew about him smoking that marijuana cigarette that had been laced with heroin. Although that had been 40 years ago, Tank still recalled the effects.

And thinking of that, Tank wondered to himself if there was some piece of his history that absolutely no one knew about, not a living or dead soul. He looked at Michael.

"Go ahead, pick something," Michael said.

"I find it very unnerving, you reading my mind. If you want to grant me a wish, I wish you'd stop," Tank said.

"You know, Tank, there are not many people on earth with whom I could converse in this manner. Most people would deny that I could read their minds, or at least put me through a series of tests. And even then, most would think it was the trick of a mage. Not you; you just jump from correct conclusion to correct conclusion. All right, I will cease reading your mind. You will have to take my word on it, though."

"It makes it a little hard to test you when you can read the answer in my mind. How 'bout if I ask you a question that I don't know the answer to?"

"Proceed," said Michael.

"Let me ask some other questions first, that you can answer. What if I went back down this mountain and told people that there was a giant who claimed to an angel up here?"

"I am most certain that won't happen. No one would believe you, for one thing. They would think you had hit your head, were suffering from a drug reaction, or you dreamed it," Michael replied, smiling.

"What if I took your picture."

"Your batteries are dead, even the spares."

"I'm having trouble convincing myself you're the real item," Tank said. "Assuming for the moment you are, what do you want?"

Michael paused for a moment as if to collect his thoughts. "We need a savior. From time to time, humans being humans, they need a religious - what you would term a 'kick in the butt' - to keep them upright and moral. This happens every thousand years or so, that we need to send a teacher out amongst the masses.

"You can probably deduce from the state of human morality at the moment that you humans need an upgrade. The United States is one of the most civilized nations on earth, and it is descending into really questionable behavior. One has only to watch 'Taxicab Confessions' to wonder about this country's perception of right and wrong. And it is worse elsewhere. When a head of state in Africa can practice cannibalism, and the world takes little notice, well, it is time for a change."

"And you want me to be the next Jesus," Tank asked.

"Jesus, Mohammed, Buddha, we do not care. You probably have noted that the major religions are pretty similar. We just want right and wrong taught, the Golden Rule, that kind of thing. We do not even have to give you any direction. Your sense of right and wrong is very well defined. All we have to give you is the power to create a miracle here and there.

Whatever you teach will catch on. We cannot force you to teach anything. I cannot even force you to sit here and listen. But the timing is getting crucial; we need to find someone, soon," Michael said.

"Why," asked Tank, genuinely curious about that aspect of Michael's pitch.

"Because you humans are about to go into space. Within a couple of hundred years, you are going to be outside the solar system. Other sentient beings live out there. You are not, as it happens, alone. We would rather not see a hedonistic, amoral, murderous, warlike race of savages out amongst the other emerging races in our galaxy. And we would rather not see you destroy yourselves, either. That remains a possibility," Michael explained.

Tank patted Rex on his head and pondered what he had been told so far. He still had no proof that Michael was what he said he was. And he couldn't think of any test that would prove it. Whatever part of his past he could use to question Michael, the alleged angel could answer by plucking the answer from Tank' s own memory. Mind reading wasn't total proof. There was enough evidence in human history that certain individuals had what were called paranormal powers. And being 15 feet tall wasn't proof; Michael could be a freak of nature. He could be Bigfoot, wandering these mountains and surviving in secret all these years.

Rex caught his attention by whimpering ever so slightly. Tank looked at the dog. Dogs try to communicate with their masters. Usually the communication is obvious, as when the dog is begging. Or when the dog has been trained to ask to go outside. Sometimes, though, the dog tries to communicate, and the human doesn't have a clue what thought the animal is trying to transmit. This was one of those times, and Rex cried in frustration. Rex almost sounded like that damn cat. Cat. Tank looked at Michael.

"What's my cat's name?"

"Your cat? The black cat with the white feet? Her name is Pounce de Leon. You named her that because you did not like your wife's names for animals - such as Fronck - and it was your turn to name the pet," Michael replied, and Tank knew from that he was the real deal. The angel couldn't have plucked that from Tank's mind because Tank hadn't been able to dredge that name out of his memory no matter how hard he tried. Ever since he realized that he couldn't remember the cat's name, he'd attributed it to some form of early Alzheimer's, the disease that had claimed his dad. He told one of his co-workers that if he heard the name, he'd know it was right, but he couldn't recall it on his own. Pounce de Leon. Now Tank was forced to seriously consider what Michael was offering - to be the next messiah.

Well, why not. Maybe this was the big karma pay back. His life seemed to be a long series of dashed hopes. As a high school sophomore, he'd lost his girl to a senior. So when he became a senior, he'd figured that couldn't happen again, except then he'd lost Joyce Kawaleski to a college guy.

He seemed to come in second in everything. The best the high school football team ever did was third place in state. He'd missed by one person a spot on the college tennis team. If he made an investment, it went bad or just sat there. If he passed up an investment, people got rich all around him. The next woman he'd fallen in love with after Joyce came home from a trip and gave him venereal disease.

"It could have been AIDS," Michael commented.

"I thought you weren't going to do that anymore," Tank said with some irritation.

"Apologies. I wanted to point out that your life also could have been quite a bit worse."

"That may be true, but it couldn't have been much worse these last four years. All I've got left in the way of honest companionship is this dog," Tank said, scratching Rex behind the knob on the top of the dog's head. Rex pushed his nose against Tank's hand, asking for more.

"So take what I offer. Many a man agonizes over the junctures in life, the choice made or not made. You have an opportunity to adopt a life in which all decisions made are correct ones. You will be loved not by one, but by millions. All you say will be heeded; all your acts will be just. You admire King Arthur? You will be King Arthur, come now to save the world, not just southern England," Michael said.

"You're a globalist," Tank commented.

"I am a minion of the Lord of All," Michael replied, "and you, by chance alone, have been groomed for this position. Why do you think you have such an odd name?"

"My father got it from some book. He read a lot."

"Actually, he chose a name no one else on earth had. Or at least he tried. He wanted his only son to be unique in at least that one way, if not in others. Like Buddha - certainly an odd, but distinctive name. Or Jesus. It is one of the attributes you have for this job. That, and you have the ability to rule," Michael said.

"Jesus didn't rule anything," Tank observed.

"That was zero A.D. In that time period, an idea could rule. Now, someone is going to have to rule in fact. What would you do with Palestine?"

Tank had thought about that. "Tell Israel to move the settlements out, or start losing American aid. Israel is totally dependent on American aid, so they'd have to listen. Give Arafat a Palestinian state on the West Bank and Gaza. Wall it off from Israel, the way they're sort of doing anyway."

"Why?"

"Cause Israel's wrong to hold on to conquered territory, and it makes us look like idiots to attack Iraq for conquering Kuwait, but support Israel after it has conquered and annexed Arab territory."

"And you like Arafat?"

"No, I think he condones terrorism. So give him his own little country. It'll fall apart in five years. Either that, or some dissident faction will kill him. Then Palestine will dissolve into chaos, and we could support some sane state to step in and take it over," Tank said, "And that's my outline for world peace."

'And if it worked, would be counted a miracle. Next stop, Nobel Peace Prize," Michael said, applauding lightly. "And it would work. You would be blessed, people would say, with the ability to deal with world leaders, to know their thoughts, their real intentions."

This was beginning to sound better and better to Tank. He'd toyed with the idea of running for office, had even been asked by some locally powerful people to do that. And he'd fantasized about being rich enough to make changes, not huge like rebuilding a country, but to restore that crumbling church in town, set up some people in business who otherwise wouldn't ever have the capital to do it, adopt a couple kids from overseas. Tank snuck a look at Michael to see if the angel was eavesdropping on his thoughts.

Michael didn't say anything; just held up his large hands in denial.

Everybody has those fantasies, Tank thought. Every kid knocked down by a bully would read those comic book ads and dream of piling on muscle and exacting revenge on the bully, and by the way, get the girl back. It's just fantasy. But how many actually have ordered the weight sets, put on the muscle, sought out the bully and beat him up? Was this one of those junctures where he was going to make the wrong decision? Was there a wrong decision?

Tank had a high IQ and an active, some would say overactive imagination. He loved to read about the ancient empires, and would put himself in the place of, say, Commodus. If Commodus had been sane, if he had been as intelligent an emperor as the five who preceded him, the Roman Empire might have survived. All it needed at that critical juncture was a great leader. Tank had often thought the U.S. was approaching that same point in its history.

Or Tank could see himself as the father of a dynasty, laying down laws - practical laws - that would have endured along with the statutes of Hammarabi or Justinian. He could imagine starting with a modest city state, such as Corinth, and leading it to a position of power in the ancient world. Or he could see himself taking over a modern third-world country and leading it into the 20th Century without making the mistakes that modern states had made when they embarked on that same journey.

Tank could see the mistakes that were made in the past. More to the point, he could see the mistakes that were being made today. And there was no risk here, no hard decision to make, no investment to be made, no money to be borrowed, no woman to choose. Or was there no risk?

"What if I refuse the offer?" he asked.

"Oh, we would have to find another," Michael said casually, but added, "That would take a long time," the angel added. "We have been grooming you for generations."

"What would happen to me?" Tank pressed.

Michael took on a pained expression. "You asked what would happen if you went down the mountain and told people what you had seen and learned up here. I said I was most certain that wouldn't happen. It cannot happen."

Tank didn't understand Michael's point for a moment, then grasped it. "Oh. If I don't accept, I won't be going down this mountain."

"But Tank, the world is before you, both literally and figuratively. Why not accept? You are perfect for this. You have been through the wilderness, if you grant that the wilderness is your life. You have been stripped of nearly all your worldly possessions. You are half into Faerie as it is, with your Tranquil Grove of the muscled branches and your Blasted Grove of the tortured limbs. You can speak as if you walked into this world from another. You would be a figure of mysticism and power. And you would actually be doing it, not lying abed and agonizing over what you should have done ten years, twenty years, thirty years ago. You are like the partygoer who walked away from an argument, and thought ten minutes later of what you should have said. I will give you a life where the retorts come out on time, on point. I would give you happiness, fulfillment!" Michael exclaimed, and for a moment, Tank was caught up in the vision. But only for a moment, because there was one more question.

"And what price would I have to pay? There's always a price," Tank said.

"A small price. You would have to go naked back into the world, as the great mystics came naked out of the wildernesses. You have been stripped of all you valued, or almost so. You would have to give up that one last minor item. For any being to get such a return, a price has to be paid," Michael said, and looked directly at the dog.

Rex looked at Michael, but only for a couple seconds, then looked at Tank and whined a little. The dog was confused by all this chatter that he couldn't understand. And he was hungry and thirsty. The man and the angel had conversed for over two hours.

"Rex has to die?" Tank asked incredulously.

"The dog has to die. It will be quick and painless. You have to walk away from the dog, retrace the track you used to climb this mountain, and do not look back. Then you will have been stripped of all worldly goods and companions, burned naked like iron enclosed in wood and dropped into the flames. The wood burns off, and the steel remains. So shall you be," Michael intoned. The angel held out his hand. "Leave the dog with me."

Rex shifted his weight from right front paw to left front paw and back, very uneasy now. He leaned against Tank's leg, unhappy with the current tone of the conversation and seeking comfort in the contact with his master. Humans may waiver in their loyalties to their dogs, but dogs have no such doubts. Rex knew his place was with Tank, wherever Tank was headed.

"Have been stripped," Tank thought. "'You have been stripped of all you valued,' Michael had said. The angel spoke very precisely, didn't even use contractions. Michael didn't say, 'You have lost all you valued.' He said, 'You have been stripped of all you valued'."

The angel spoke in the passive voice that allowed the speaker to describe an action without identifying the actor. Otherwise, Michael would have said, "He stripped you of all you valued," or, "We stripped you of all you valued."

It wasn't me that made all those wrong decisions; it was a higher power that made them wrong. The big games he had lost, the women who had left him, the jobs he hadn't gotten, the investments that had gone bad; all circumstances that could have been manipulated by a higher power, such as...Michael. And he's still reading my mind!

Michael sighed and leaned back against the rock. "So look at it from a practical standpoint. We trained you. We led you to this point. You can handle the job. You want goodness? Be good. The offer remains. Think of it as power politics, just like you described with Palestine. The Angels perceive a threat, and we go take care of it. You are the current solution. And you have the advantage of knowing how capable we can be. So bargain. We don't really have time to create another like you. Humans are in space. You are learning too many things too fast. What kind of people do you want to see go out to the stars? Those led by totalitarian dictators, or those led by democracies?"

Something occurred to Tank. "Why don't you just do it yourself? You said you could make yourself look like anything you wanted, like a 15-foot tall yuppie hiker. Why don't you make yourself a handsome, unemployed lawyer with a blond wife and 1.7 kids. That would fit most of our presidential candidates."

"We have limitations," Michael replied.

"Like in the Bible? Why did angels have to work through humans? What other little problems do you encounter when trying to manipulate a race like ours?" Tank said. "Seems to me there were two kinds of angels, those sent by God, and those kicked out of heaven, the fallen kind. The Bible might have gone through multiple translations over several thousand years, but the gist of it is the same - the struggle by greater beings for the human soul."

"You are jumping to conclusions," Michael replied.

"But I do that, you said. I jump from correct conclusion to correct conclusion. I wonder who you really are," Tank said. "You are offering me total power. Would the U.S. be a democracy when I was through? I wonder if I would be a Jesus, or if I would be a Stalin."

And now he was afraid. He was perched on a very high place across from a very powerful being, a being who seemed to transform before his eyes from a benevolent giant into a malevolent monster. Tank was no small man, but a fight with Michael would be no fight. Tank would be killed.

Never go to a bad place without a big dog, he thought. Somebody had told him that. Whenever you got into trouble, the trouble wasn't as bad if you had a big dog beside you. Clearly, the Galactics, or whoever they were, had tried to kill Rex. There had been the irrigation pipe incident, the night in the wilderness when the dog inexplicably had gotten lost, the near-miss with the moose, getting hit by a truck. His friends had told him Rex must be part cat, to have survived all that unscathed.

He'd always thought dogs were a special kind of creature that maybe some higher being had put on this earth to take care of an unstable mankind. Dogs were stable. They were loyal, they were brave, they were incapable of dishonesty. They were the Knights of the Round Table of the animal kingdom. And Rex was a perfect example of his species. Perfect.

"You can't touch this dog, can you?" Tank said to Michael. "There's a grain of truth in the Bible. We call you angels. You say you're some sort of citizen of the galaxy. But you're limited, for whatever 'technical' reason. This dog's good; you're evil. Here's the real test: kill the dog. You don't have my permission. I stand by him, as I promised him I would. But kill him if you can. If you're the wrong sort of angel, I don't think you can touch a spirit so pure," Tank said, wrapping his arms around the big head of his dog. Rex tried to lick his face; the dog felt better for the gesture.

Michael's face contorted in a grimace of rage for an instant, then relaxed into the set recognition of defeat. "I cannot kill the dog, but I can kill you. That is the price to be paid for making naught of a project - you - that consumed 200 years," Michael said, rising to his full 15 feet of height.

"No one's ever turned you down before?" Tank asked, rising himself to meet the threat.

"They have, but you have never heard of them, as none shall ever hear of you," Michael said, striding forward and raising Tank up in his massive arms. The fallen angel heaved Tank over the side of the peak, and Tank slid rapidly down the steep slope toward the near-vertical face of the cliff, unable to gain purchase on the sliding rocks.

Rex, whom Michael could not touch, leaped over the rock and chased Tank at full speed down the steep slope. The dog caught up to the man at the edge. Tank managed to grab onto Rex's collar as both of them went over the precipice. The only thing Tank could hold onto as he fell was his dog, and he drew the animal to him and held him tightly. It was such a long fall that Tank was able to think to himself, and to his dog, "Neither of us will die before the other."

No one ever found them there beneath the cliff, man and dog together among the green trees below the Divide that marked the spine of a continent. The cascade of rocks that followed their fall buried them under jagged, unmarked headstones of granite, as if the mountain itself had arranged the funeral. There were huge fires the following summer that roared through that area, but the grove in which Rex and Tank died never burned. The grove took on an odd aspect, its trees different from the surrounding forest. Scores of years later, a hiker who followed paths apart from the frequently trodden trails remarked to herself that it seemed this grove of trees had a nobility about it - straight, thick, well-formed trees, unbending against the merciless weather of these parts. Stolid Grove, she called it, and then asked herself why she had felt compelled to give it a name. The hiker gazed at the grove with admiration and some curiosity for several minutes, then walked on.

About the Author

Jim Dustin lives way, way back in the mountains of Colorado where he hikes, camps, fishes, snowshoes, skates, skis and otherwise enjoys the hell out of the most beautiful land in the west. Before that, he spent 25 years in Missouri, and before that, 18 years in Wisconsin. Mr. Dustin is an accomplished writer who has won many awards for his nonfiction writing over a 30-year career as a journalist. He began writing these stories to comfort a friend who was fond, perhaps overly fond of her dogs. It's hard for us to lose our best friends, but Mr. Dustin imagines that there might be another calling for these dogs after that sad event.

Printed in the United States
16466LVS00003B/130-234